LIMOS OUTLAWS

Lieutenant Rand receives an unusual request to travel to Mexico and map out previously uncharted territory, but all too soon he finds that the task is fraught with danger. Captured by a group of bandits led by Jose del Monte, Rand is forced to undergo marriage to the beautiful but disfigured Alicia. Seeing an opportunity to escape from the outlaws' hideout, Rand and Alicia take it and flee to the poppy fields. Here, Rand encounters the villainous Scarpia and his operation supplying opium to the Army. With help from unexpected sources, Rand embarks on a final shoot-out amongst the white poppies.

LIMOS OUTLAWS

LIMOS OUTLAWS

by

Ron Watkins

Dales Large Print Books
Long Preston, North Yorkshire,
BD23 4ND, England.

British Library Cataloguing in Publication Data.

Watkins, Ron
Limos outlaws.

A catalogue record of this book is
available from the British Library

ISBN   1-84262-487-3 pbk
ISBN   978-1-84262-487-6 pbk

First published in Great Britain in 2005 by
Robert Hale Limited

Published in Large Print 2006 by arrangement with
Robert Hale Limited

Dales Large Print is an imprint of Library Magna Books Ltd.

Printed and bound in Great Britain by
T.J. (International) Ltd., Cornwall, PL28 8RW

For my granddaughters – the twins,
Katy and Rebecca Watkins

CHAPTER 1

Lieutenant Clive Rand stood stiffly to attention.

'Stand at ease, Lieutenant,' said his commanding officer, Colonel Stanton.

They were in the officer's room. The colonel, who was seated behind his desk, cleared his throat.

Rand realized that it was rather an awkward moment for his superior officer. He had been summoned to appear before him as soon as he had returned to the army post where he was stationed.

'I – er – have to offer my sincere condolences,' the colonel began. 'Of course I met Martha a couple of times at staff functions. She was a lovely lady.' He coughed again. 'A lovely lady.'

Rand said nothing. There was nothing

really to add to the colonel's brief eulogy. His wife, Martha, had been a lovely lady. That was how he would always remember her.

'You've had a month's compassionate leave,' said the colonel. 'Are you ready to resume your duties?'

'Yes, sir.'

'Good.' The colonel sounded relieved. He coughed again.

I wonder what's coming this time, thought Rand. His superior officer's coughs were usually an indication that he had something important to announce.

'I've got a rather unusual duty for you to perform,' the colonel began. 'It's not strictly in our line of duty in the training post. But from time to time we do have strange requests from headquarters.' He glanced at a sheet of paper which lay on his desk. Rand waited for some indication about what this strange duty would be.

'It says here that in your previous experience, before joining the army, you were a surveyor. That you mapped the

10

Cheyenne Mountains for the Clancey railroad company. It was essential that they had accurate maps before knowing whether it was feasible for them to build the railroad. It also says here that as a result of your survey, they were able successfully to build the railroad.'

'I believe my maps helped, sir,' Rand conceded.

'It's rather strange for someone who's a surveyor to join the army.'

'There are only a few railroads being built in this part of the country,' said Rand. 'Most of them are being built in the North and in the West. I'd rather stay here in the South. And, of course, it was Martha's home as well.'

The colonel nodded. He, too, was from the South and could entirely sympathize with Rand.

'The request I've had is for someone with a surveyor's experience to assess whether it is feasible to build a railway.' He coughed again.

Where were they going to send him? He had already indicated that he didn't want to go up north. He was a Southerner born and bred. His father had fought on the side of the Confederates during the Civil War. True, they had lost, but it had left him with an unreasoning dislike for anything north of the Mason-Dixon line.

'It says here,' the colonel tapped the sheet of paper, 'that you speak Spanish.'

'My grandmother was Spanish,' said Rand. 'I've got aunts and uncles living in San Caldiz.'

The colonel studied him. Maybe he is searching for some sign of Spanish blood in me, thought Rand.

When the colonel's announcement about the nature of the mission came it took him completely by surprise. 'We have a request from the Mexican government to send a surveyor to see whether it will be feasible to run a railway from San Caldiz to Limos.' His superior officer gave him a few seconds to absorb his statement. Then he continued:

'Of course you don't have to comply with this request. We can easily send a telegram to headquarters saying that we have no one on our staff who would be suitable for this mission. The decision is entirely yours.'

'Can I have some time to think about it, sir?'

'Come back to see me this afternoon and let me know your decision.'

Rand returned early in the afternoon.

'I'll take the mission,' he announced.

CHAPTER 2

A couple of days later Rand was sitting in an office which was considerably more opulent than the colonel's. It belonged to Pedro Castales, the mayor of San Caldiz.

'I am very pleased that the United States government has seen fit to send somebody with experience to survey the possibility of building our railway,' said the mayor. 'If it will be possible to build it from here to Limos, it will open up a new world for that town. It will bring a new prosperity to the area. It will bring in Americans like yourself. It will be the dawn of a new era. I believe you have been to San Caldiz before.'

'My grandmother was Mexican. She came from this town.'

The mayor, too, subjected him to the same stare as his colonel. He obviously couldn't find any trace of Rand's Spanish ancestory for he gave an expressive shrug.

'So you've got some knowledge of our countryside. Have you ever been to Limos?'

'No.' Rand shook his head.

'Right. Let's get down to business.' The mayor rubbed his hands. 'Is there anything you will need on your travels?'

'I've brought all my equipment with me. The only things I'll need will be food and drink. How far is it from here to Limos?'

'Thirteen miles. The trouble is that there are some mountains between the two towns.'

'So we'd be talking of tunnelling through them?'

'Unless you think it would be better to go round them. One other thing is that this expedition must have total secrecy. If the landowners who live between here and Limos find out the true reason for your survey they will increase the price they would be asking for their land. The result would be the costs would rise dramatically. It would probably make the whole project a non-starter.'

'You can rely on my discretion,' stated Rand.

Rand arranged to take ten days' supplies with him. He had no idea how long the task would take, but ten days sounded reasonable. He also stabled his horse. The standard cavalry horse which he had ridden to San Caldiz, while ideal for eating up the miles on a flat terrain, would be of little use in the mountains. He therefore chose a small mountain-pony. His tall frame looked

15

out of place on the pony, but he knew that the horse would be able to negotiate the mountain trails far more certainly than the horse he left behind in the stables.

The first part of his task was almost embarrassingly simple. He rode along a flat plain towards Limos. From time to time he stopped to take samples of the soil. He found that underneath the sparse layer of soil was a firm base of clay. It would be ideal for laying railroad lines on.

This ideal terrain lasted for four miles. When it came to an end the change was dramatic. He found that he was suddenly confronted by a steep mountain range. Not only was it steep but it rose up to what he estimated to be roughly 3,000 feet. The only consolation he found when he examined the mountains was that they seemed to be of limestone, which made making a tunnel through them a possibility. If they had been made of granite then the possibility of a tunnel would be far less feasible.

Having ascertained the composition of the

rocks he prepared to spend the night on the plain. It would be his last night, since the next day he would have to start climbing the mountain. Not that the prospect daunted him. Once in the mountains he would be able to indulge his favourite hobby – map-making. He doubted whether anyone had ever made any maps of the mountains. So here was his chance.

In fact the mountains were higher than he had thought. He calculated that they were more like 5,000 feet high rather than his original estimate of 3,000 feet. Even in this latitude, which was not too far from the equator, he could distinguish the snow on top of the mountain range.

On the third day tragedy struck. He was riding the pony along a path when a mountain adder reared up and struck at it. The pony screamed with fright. Rand shot the adder but the pony was soon rolling on the path in agony. Rand had no choice but to shoot it, too.

From then on his progress had to be on

foot. This meant that it was slower. Not that it particularly bothered him. He knew that he was heading in the direction of Limos. He took his map-readings and drew his maps as he moved slowly forward.

Only one thing did trouble him. When the mayor of San Caldiz had given him his parting words of advice he threw in the casual remark that there were some outlaws in the mountains. He added that they shouldn't bother him because he wouldn't be venturing that high up in the mountains. But in order to complete his drawings of the maps Rand was forced to climb higher and higher.

On the tenth day of his travels tragedy struck again.

CHAPTER 3

There was no doubt about it, he was in trouble. In fact he would say that his position at the moment was definitely less than healthy. He was about 3,000 feet above sea-level in what was loosely termed outlaw country. Ten minutes before he had slipped while perched on a narrow ledge in order to take a map-reading. The result of the slip was that his ankle now hurt, but, more important, he had lost his compass. He had seen it merrily roll down the mountainside when he had slipped. At a guess it now nestled 1,000 feet below him and there was no way on earth he could reclaim it.

He sat on a rock while he scanned the uninviting scenery around him. Mostly it consisted of bleached limestone with only sparse tufts of grass here and there clinging to hollows. He wondered what were his chances of arriving at Limos before nightfall. He stood up and tested his suspect ankle. To move only a few paces made him wince with pain. He didn't think he had broken anything, but he had definitely sprained it. So that seemed to solve the problem whether he would reach Limos before nightfall – the answer was certainly no.

Not that another night on the mountains particularly worried him – he was used to sleeping out in the open. What did concern him though was the fact that his food rations had been almost completely used up. So far he had spent ten days on the mountains taking his map-readings. He had thought originally that he would spend a week on his task, but because of the features of the terrain, with its numerous dry valleys and ridges, his progress had been much slower than he had expected.

He glanced up at the sun. He knew that Limos lay to the south-east. By keeping the sun on his right he could proceed roughly in the right direction. He strapped his pack on to his back and prepared to set out again. At least when he eventually arrived in Limos he would be able to confirm that his days spent in the mountains had been worthwhile. He had mapped an area of Mexico that nobody had mapped before. He had made dozens of drawings. He had checked that the mountains indeed consisted of limestone, which would make tunnelling through them a relatively simple matter.

In that respect his journey had been worth while, but had it helped to fill the void he had experienced when his beloved wife of twelve years, Martha, had died? He knew that nothing would completely fill it. The only thing he could hope for was that the ache would become less as time passed.

He started to climb the long ridge that lay ahead. Rather, he started to hobble up it. It was about 500 yards in length and he had no idea what lay beyond it. Probably another similar ridge, he decided. His ankle was hurting like hell. He wished he had a

21

stick to help him take the weight off it. But the only trees growing on this white wilderness were those he had left behind this morning a thousand or so feet below. He glanced up at the sky. The sun was its usual mocking yellow ball. The only consolation was that, because he was 3,000 feet up, its heat wasn't as overpowering as if he had been down on the plain.

After a painful half an hour or so of climbing he reached the top of the ridge. He wondered whether he would be able to see Limos from it. He breasted the ridge and saw, not Limos, but a group of outlaws sitting on the ground. Their reactions were quicker than his as the speed with which they produced their revolvers testified.

'Ah, *señor*,' said one. 'Please join us. But first I must ask you to give up your revolver.'

Rand complied. After all, this *was* outlaw country, he reflected ruefully.

CHAPTER 4

The outlaws' camp was in a large hollow about half a mile from where Rand had come across them. One of the dozen or so outlaws, noticing that Rand was having difficulty in walking, kindly lent him the stick he was carrying. It made Rand's progress easier, and he was now able to keep up with the rest – without the constant jab of a revolver in his ribs reminding him to do so.

When they reached the camp Rand was surprised how many tents were in it. There must be at least fifty, he thought; it was more like a village than an outlaw camp. Many of the inhabitants came out to see him as he was ushered into a space in the middle of the camp. A chair was brought and Rand thankfully sank into it.

A Mexican whom Rand assumed was the

leader of the outlaws sat opposite him. The Mexican was seated in an old armchair to suit his status. He was a typical Mexican with swarthy skin and a large moustache. He was the sort of man whom women would describe as handsome.

'My name is Jose,' he announced, in English.

'Clive Rand,' supplied Rand.

'What are you doing in our part of the world, Mr Rand?' asked the Mexican.

By now the crowd around Rand and his interrogator had swollen to a few dozen. Many of them were children. Rand noticed that they did not seem to be particularly undernourished, in fact they appeared to be the sort of children you would expect to find in a prosperous town like San Caldiz.

'You haven't answered my question,' said Jose.

'I'm making maps,' said Rand.

'You're making maps,' repeated the Mexican slowly. 'Take your pack off,' he commanded.

Rand did so. Jose signalled to one of his men to open it. Rand saw his few possessions tipped out on to the ground. Anger boiled in him as the Mexican spread them out. They were his change of clothes, his drawing-book, his copy of *The Life of Wellington*, his meagre rations, the bag containing his theodolite and his folding telescope.

Jose's eyes lit up when he saw the telescope.

'If what you say is true,' he said, 'why do you want the telescope?'

'I use it for drawing maps.'

'You were using it to help you to spy on us,' said Jose, opening out the telescope and looking through it. 'It is a very good telescope. I can see miles with it.' So saying he surveyed the mountainside.

'I've already told you. I use it for drawing my maps.'

'That is a very good cover for someone whose real purpose is to spy on us,' said Jose.

'Why should I want to spy on you?'

25

demanded Rand. 'I didn't know you existed until I stumbled across you up on the mountain.'

'So you say,' said Jose. 'But of course you *would* say that, wouldn't you?' There was a hidden threat in his statement. The Mexican who had tipped out Rand's belongings was thumbing through his drawing-book. 'Have you found anything, Santos?' asked Jose.

'No, only drawings of the mountains,' answered Santos.

'I've already told you that,' snapped Rand.

Jose stared at him thoughtfully. Rand was aware that he was sweating, partly because of the heat, and partly because the expression on Jose's face indicated that he was not a happy man. In fact it was definitely the expression of a man who was displeased with the answers he was receiving from the *gringo* in front of him.

'Tie him up,' commanded Jose.

Half a dozen men quickly stepped forward. The first one was surprised by a solid straight right to the chin as Rand moved quickly for a big man. The second hesitated a fraction too long on seeing his companion being floored. The split-second delay caused him the same treatment, as he too became the victim of one of Rand's punches – this time a left hook. However Rand's flurry of activity which helped to get the frustration out of his system came to an abrupt end when one of his attackers stepped quickly behind him and hit him with the butt of his pistol. Rand sank down into blackness.

CHAPTER 5

When Rand recovered he realized he was lying on a straw mattress in a tent. He also realized that his head hurt. There was someone else in the tent – a woman, who had her back to him. He groaned.

'Are you conscious?' she asked, still with her back to him.

'I think so.' The effort of speaking caused him to groan involuntarily again.

'I'm going to give you something to drink,' she said.

'That'll be nice.' He tried turning his head so that he could catch a glimpse of her face, but the effort started his head aching again.

'There's one thing,' she said as she poured some water from a jar.

'What's that?'

'When you look at me you're going to have a shock.'

'In what way?'

'One side of my face is disfigured. It was burned a few months ago.'

Even though she had prepared him for her disfiguration, when she handed him the glass of water, he couldn't refrain from an involuntary shudder.

'It's all right,' she said, 'I'm used to the reaction.'

She said it in a flat, unemotional voice but behind the remark Rand sensed that there were months of unhappiness.

'I'm no oil-painting myself,' said Rand. 'And anyhow it's what's inside a person that counts, not what's on the outside.'

There was enough light in the tent through the half-open flap for Rand to see her face quite clearly. The whole of one side of her face was disfigured. The other side was quite attractive. Her other redeeming feature was her hair, which was thick and wavy and black.

'Thanks for the water,' said Rand.

'You were a fool trying to take on half a dozen of Jose's men,' she said, as she watched him drink.

'I know. I couldn't stand the sight of that member of the gang emptying my possessions all over the place.'

'They're over there,' she said, pointing to a corner of the tent where his pack stood. 'It's all there.'

'Thanks,' he said. 'I don't even know your name to thank you properly.'

'Alicia,' she replied.

'That's a...' he was going to say pretty

name, but realized that any reference to prettiness could be hurtful to her, '...name I'll always remember,' he ended, lamely.

'And what's your name?' she demanded.

'Clive Rand,' he replied.

'Well, Clive, the committee are deciding at this moment what they are going to do with you.'

'They seem to think I was a spy,' said Rand. 'If I were a spy who would I be spying for?'

'Why, Alphonso of course,' said Alicia. The surprise in her tone indicated that she thought he would have known that.

'Alphonso,' said Rand, thoughtfully. 'Isn't he the person who's the mayor of Limos?'

'You don't have to pretend to me,' she said, beginning to get angry. 'I don't care whether you're a spy or not. Although I wouldn't like to see you hanged,' she added.

'Thanks,' said Rand, drily. 'But I can assure you I am not a spy. I just happened to be someone who was passing by.'

'Passing by – up in these mountains?' she

said scornfully.

'I was making a map. It's a hobby of mine,' explained Rand.

'They say it was a cover for your spying.'

'Whose side are you on?' demanded Rand, irritably. Her continued scepticism was making his head ache abominably again.

'The meeting's taking a long time,' she said, thoughtfully.

'Is that a good sign or a bad one?' demanded Rand.

'I don't know.' She leaned over him to give him a fresh glass of water. As she did so she caught sight of the chain hanging around his neck. 'Are you a Catholic?' she asked.

'No,' he replied curtly; then he realised that she had seen the chain hanging round his neck. 'This is my identification,' he explained.

'What do you mean?' she asked, puzzled.

He took the chain off and handed it to her.

'I'm an army officer.'

'Why didn't you tell them you were an American officer?' she demanded.

'They didn't give me much of a chance,' he pointed out.

At that moment a Mexican wearing a bedraggled soldier's uniform stepped inside the tent.

'Jose wants to see you,' he said, curtly.

'Can't you see he's not well,' said Alicia, sharply.

'He's well enough to answer a few questions,' retorted the Mexican. He put his arm around Rand and hauled him to his feet. Rand pushed the Mexican away. He was determined to go under his own steam even though his head was aching abominably. The Mexican guided him to the next tent and pushed him inside. Rand managed to keep his balance with an effort.

There were about half a dozen Mexicans in the tent. They were all squatting on the floor except for Jose who was seated on a wooden chair.

'Who are you, and what are you doing in these mountains?' Jose asked.

'I'm Clive Rand. Lieutenant Clive Rand,'

said Clive, emphatically.

Puzzlement flickered on Jose's face.

'An officer in the army?' he demanded.

'That's right,' replied Rand, curtly.

The puzzlement on Jose's face changed to outright surprise. He recovered his composure slowly.

'Can you prove it?'

Rand unwound the chain from around his neck.

'Here's my badge of office,' he stated.

One of the Mexicans took it from him and handed it to Jose, who examined it carefully before handing it back to Rand.

'This makes a difference,' the Mexican who had brought Rand in pointed out. 'We don't want any trouble with the American army.'

'Don't be stupid, Paco,' snapped Jose. 'If he is a real officer then the chances are they don't know where he is. And anyhow we're thirty miles away from America. You don't think they've got cannons that can fire that distance, do you?'

'Well, what are we going to do with him?' demanded Paco.

'I haven't decided yet,' said Jose. He stared thoughtfully at Rand.

'I suggest you let me go,' said Rand. 'I'll walk out of here and put it down to experience.'

'And as soon as you get to Limos you'll tell Alphonso where we are hiding. You could even lead him and his army back here,' sneered Jose.

'When I get away from here I'm going straight back over the border,' snapped Rand. 'I've had enough of these mountains – and of you scum,' he added.

Jose scowled. For a fleeting moment Rand wondered whether he had gone too far.

However the tension was broken by the arrival of Alicia.

'What are you going to do with him?' she demanded.

'This is men's work,' said Jose, sharply. 'Get out.'

Alicia moved protectively nearer Rand.

'He's not a spy. You can't hang him,' she cried.

'I said get out,' snarled Jose. He nodded almost imperceptibly to Paco who swung his fist at Alicia, hitting her full in the face.

Rand's reaction was probably slower than normal due to having his weight on the wrong foot in order to ease his aching ankle. He stepped forward to hit Paco with a right hook, but the 'click' of the hammer on a revolver which Jose had suddenly produced reminded him that his instinctive reaction should be postponed for the moment.

'So you wish to stand up for this gringo?' demanded Jose with a smirk.

'He hasn't done anything wrong,' protested Alicia. 'Except in coming to this place,' she added, bitterly.

'Maybe you like this gringo,' suggested Jose, his smile widening with every word.

He was clearly trying to goad Alicia into a reply, but she said nothing. She contented herself with dabbing with her handkerchief the cut in her cheek which had been caused by Paco's fist.

'Maybe you would like to marry this gringo,' announced Jose, delivering his *coup de gras* with a delighted smile.

'Don't be ridiculous,' snapped Rand.

'Ah, you're already married?' Jose raised an enquiring eyebrow.

'No, I'm not,' snapped Rand. 'And I'm not marrying anyone,' he added emphatically.

'Not even the beautiful Alicia,' sneered Paco.

Rand stepped forward with the obvious intention of hitting him, but a reciprocal movement from Jose's gun stopped him in his tracks.

'It's your choice, gringo,' purred Jose. 'You can either marry the desirable Alicia, or we will hang you as a spy. The decision, I would think, is not a difficult one.'

CHAPTER 6

Five minutes later Rand was again lying in the bed in Alicia's tent. This time he was alone in the tent. Alicia had made herself scarce without saying a word when they left Jose's tent after he had delivered his ultimatum. Rand was alone with his thoughts which were not particularly cheerful ones.

It was obvious that Jose was harbouring doubts about whether he was a spy or not. Although to all appearances Jose was a small-time bandit leader, he was far from stupid. He had realized that once Rand left the camp, he would head straight for Limos. Even if Rand was not in Alphonso's pay as a spy he would make a point of getting in contact with Alphonso if only to pay Jose back for the ill-treatment he had received in the bandit's camp. Rand would divulge the whereabouts of the camp, and the so-far secret hiding-place would be revealed. In fact Rand, having been engaged in making maps, would be able to pin-point the exact location of the camp's site.

Therefore Rand had to be kept in the camp. Of course the easy option would be for him to remain in the camp as a corpse. This would solve the problem of having Rand reveal the whereabouts of the camp, since corpses were not particularly active in divulging information. On the other hand Rand was an officer in the United States army. And it was a well-known fact that the army looked after their own. If Rand failed to return to his camp, then it was reasonable to assume that an army patrol would come searching for him. And that could cause Jose considerably more problems.

On the other hand, forcing Rand to marry Alicia would keep him in the camp. Probably Jose would emphasize the point that if she let him stray any distance from the camp her own life would be forfeit. So when they got married she would be an ever-present wife.

What a mess. What a God almighty mess! And it all arose because he had taken some time from surveying the railway route to indulge in his hobby of map-making. His depressing thoughts were interrupted by the arrival of Alicia.

She smiled at him. Rand tried to deduce whether it was the smile of a future wife regarding her husband-to-be. Still, he reasoned, whatever happened it wasn't her fault. She was as much a pawn in Jose's game as he was.

She came across to sit on the bed.

'You're going to marry me, aren't you?' she asked, shyly.

'I haven't got any choice, have I?' demanded Rand.

'It won't be as bad as you think,' she said. 'I won't keep you to your marriage vows. We won't be a proper husband and wife. Some time later, when your ankle is better we'll try and find a way for you to leave the camp.'

He looked at her with new-found hope. In the semi-darkness of the tent her skin blemish was not so apparent. She had a nice, pleasing voice. Probably she had been educated at a convent school. If they had to spend a few days together it might not be too bad after all.

'What happens now?' he asked, with resignation.

'We get married tomorrow. You will stay in this tent until then. Of course there will be a guard outside,' she added.

'Of course,' said Rand, drily.

'I suppose you'd rather be dead,' she said, with an unexpected flash of anger.

He took her hand.

'I seem to have got myself into a mess,' he confessed. 'The only thing I can do, as you say, is to go along with it.'

Jose chose that moment to come into the tent. He glanced at the two of them sitting on the bed.

'It's nice to see you two lovebirds getting on together,' he said, with a smirk.

'What do you want?' asked Rand, with a scowl.

'I've just come to tell you about your wedding arrangements for tomorrow. We're going to turn it into a fiesta. We don't have many chances of having a big celebration up here in the mountains, so we're going to make up for it tomorrow. There'll be wine, women and song.' He rubbed his hands together in eager anticipation of the event. 'You're honoured, gringo, that we're doing all this for you,' he added, as he turned and left the tent.

CHAPTER 7

Surprisingly Rand slept like a log after Alicia left the tent. When he awoke the first light of dawn was beginning to filter into the tent. The bridegroom had a good night's sleep, he thought ruefully, as he got up and yawned and stretched.

He put his head outside the tent. As he had expected, the guard was there.

'I want some hot water to wash and shave,' he said. 'And be quick about it,' he added.

The guard, as if recognizing someone who was used to being obeyed, moved off quickly to a large tent a short distance away.

After he had washed and shaved Rand surveyed himself in the small mirror.

Well, you certainly didn't expect you would be getting married when you started climbing these mountains, he addressed his image. However it won't be a real marriage. He contented himself with that thought as he finished shaving.

In a short while there were signs of activity outside. Coloured ribbons were being hung from some of the tents. Some wooden baths appeared and young children were being unwillingly scrubbed in them – probably their first thorough wash for weeks, Rand decided uncharitably. A small group of musicians had materialized and were practising energetically if tunelessly in a corner of the camp. The whole scene had a comic air about it which Rand would have found diverting in normal circumstances. But these were not normal circumstances, he was reminded as Jose approached the tent.

'Ah, I see that you are making sure that all the wedding arrangements are satisfactory,' he said, with a smirk.

Rand swore one day that he would get even with Jose for the indignities which he had so far suffered and probably for others to come. He remembered a line from Shakespeare. *Had all his hairs been lives my great revenge had stomach for them all.* Well he, Rand, had the stomach for revenge. As Jose would certainly find out one day after he had survived this farce. He said nothing.

'You will be pleased to know that everything about the marriage will be legal,' continued Jose. 'We have a priest in the camp who will perform the ceremony in accordance with the law.'

Rand made one last attempt to get himself out of the situation.

'If you let me go, I swear on the Bible that I will go straight back to my camp over the border. Your quarrel with whoever rules Limos has got nothing to do with me. I'm just an army officer who makes maps as a hobby.'

He realized immediately that the plea had been in vain. Jose's face darkened.

'I don't believe you,' he snarled. 'Nobody in their right senses would come to this god-forsaken part of the world unless he had another reason for coming here.'

Jose turned on his heel and stormed off. Rand went back inside the tent. Shortly afterwards he was brought a plateful of delicious tortillas. He had forgotten how hungry he was, but the smell of the tortillas reminded him. He devoured them greedily.

The Mexican who had brought the tortillas stood inside the tent watching him. He had the saddest face Rand had ever seen.

'My name is Pedro,' he announced. 'I will be the best man at your wedding. That is, unless you have any other choice,' he concluded apologetically.

'No, it's all right,' said Rand. 'You'll do. Tell me, who makes these delicious tortillas?'

'My wife,' said Pedro, proudly. 'She is the best cook in the camp. Would you like some more, *señor?*' he asked, having observed how quickly Rand had dispatched them.

Rand hesitated. Should he have some more, or not? Well, after all, they were delicious. And it was his wedding-day wasn't it?

'Tell her I would be delighted to taste some more of her excellent tortillas.'

'I will fetch them, *señor*,' said Pedro, with a delighted grin.

'What time's the wedding?' Rand asked when he returned with the tortillas.

'It will be after the siesta this afternoon,' Pedro informed him. 'There will be a fiesta. It will be the best fiesta we have ever had here. Is there anything you need before that?'

'No, I'll just meditate and think how lucky I've been,' said Rand, sarcastically.

The remark sailed ineffectually over Pedro's head.

'I'll be back later, *señor*,' he said.

Rand went back inside the tent. He stretched out on the bed. For someone who was going to receive a public humiliation in a few hours' time he felt curiously calm. There was no doubt in his mind that he would be the laughing-stock in the centre of the event. Well, he'd go along with the sham until he could find a chance to escape from this god-forsaken place.

He slept for several hours. He was awakened by the sound of gunfire.

He put his head outside the tent. Pedro materialized by his side.

'It was only some of the soldiers letting off steam,' he explained. 'They are getting ready for the fiesta.' He left the tent as another figure stepped inside. Rand assumed he was the padre, judging by the grubby dog-collar he was wearing.

'I'm Mendez. I'm marrying you,' said the newcomer, holding out his hand diffidently.

'I'm Rand.' He shook the hand cautiously, wondering whether it was rather less grubby than the padre's collar.

'I haven't done this for years,' Mendez confided. As he did so he leaned forward and delivered a strong blast of tequila in Rand's direction.

Rand stood up. He towered over the Mexican.

'I think we'd better go outside,' he suggested.

Outside the activity was continuing. Women wearing colourful costumes were hurrying here and there. Many of them glanced curiously at him as they passed. Some of the younger women stared insolently as they appraised him.

Mendez sat on the ground and Rand joined him.

'What time is the wedding?' demanded Rand.

'When Jose announces it,' answered Mendez.

Alicia's tent was on the edge of the camp. It probably reflected her insignificance in the bandits' hierarchy, Rand reflected, as he idly began whittling a stick that he had found on the ground. Mendez surreptitiously produced a bottle of tequila from his trouser-pocket. He offered it to Rand, who shook his head.

'It's for my chest,' he said, taking a deep pull. 'Most of us hate living up here in the mountains. We were not made for this life. We belong on the plain where the weather is always hot.'

'Why don't you leave this place and go back to Limos?' asked Rand.

'Because we will all be hung in the market-place,' said Mendez, simply.

'Yes, that does seem a good reason,' said Rand thoughtfully, as he continued whittling.

'Alphonso is Jose's cousin,' continued the other. 'They are sworn enemies. There is a price of twenty thousand American dollars on Jose's head.'

'How did you get mixed up with these bandits?' asked Rand casually, as he regarded the stick he had been whittling. Satisfied, he cut two notches in it.

'Three years ago we all lived in Limos. We were all happy then. Then Alphonso and his men attacked us. At that time they were the *bandidos*. They drove us out of the town. We were forced to live up here. And we've been living here ever since.'

Rand sought a diversion from Mendez's troubles by whistling to the youth who had been watching him to come over.

'Fetch me some water,' he commanded. The boy scurried away.

'Where's Alicia?' asked Rand.

'In her sister's tent. It's bad luck for a bridegroom to see a bride before the wedding.'

'I've had enough bad luck as it is,' said Rand. 'Another slice or two won't make any difference.'

The boy returned with a saucer of water. Rand proceeded to soak the bark on the stick, leaving a small gap at the end. He then began to tap the wet bark with the handle of his penknife. When it was pliable enough he slid it off the stick. He enlarged the two holes and slid the bark back on. He was now holding a whistle in his hand. To demonstrate its potential he blew two notes on it. They were clear, and penetrating. The boy watched admiringly as Rand repeated the performance. The boy's expression changed to delight when Rand tossed him the whistle.

'You can keep it,' said Rand.

Mendez took another swig from his bottle.

'How much longer will Jose keep us waiting?' demanded Rand.

'It won't be long now,' said Mendez.

His forecast proved to be right, since ten minutes later from somewhere in the camp a bell began to toll.

'We brought the bell with us from the church in Limos,' said Mendez.

Rand found that the whole population of the camp were issuing from their tents and heading towards the open space in the centre. He and Mendez joined them. Jose came over.

'Don't be miserable, gringo,' he said heartily, 'Your face is almost as sad as Pedro's.'

'I know what I'd like to do with your face,' said Rand, shaping his hand into a fist.

'Don't go too far,' said Jose, threateningly. 'Or you'll end up as dead as that ox.' He pointed to an ox hanging on a spit.

'If you do kill me don't you think the army will come looking for me?' demanded Rand. 'They know exactly where I am,' he lied.

'They can't possibly know where you are,' stated Jose. 'Anyhow, I have a plan to keep them away from here.'

'What's that?' demanded a curious Rand.

'I suppose there's no harm in telling you. After the ceremony you will write a letter to the army telling them that you have changed nationalities. You will tell them that you have now become a Mexican and that you have taken a Mexican wife. I will send them a copy of the marriage certificate to prove it.'

'Do you think I will do it?' demanded Rand, scornfully.

'Oh, yes, you will sign it,' said Jose, positively. 'Otherwise I will shoot Alicia. You may not love her, but I'm sure you would not wish to see her killed.'

'You bastard.' This time Rand stepped forward threateningly.

Jose stood his ground.

'So you see,' he said calmly, 'As you say in your country, I hold all the aces.'

The tension gradually ebbed away from Rand as he admitted the truth of Jose's statement. He took a deep breath and tried to relax. He had faced all kinds of people in his rise in the army to become one of the youngest lieutenants. He had dealt with rogues, bullies, liars, thieves, insubordinates, and all kinds of other scum. But he had never met anyone who aroused such hatred in him as Jose. If it hadn't been for the threat to Alicia he would have taken a chance and smashed his fist into Jose's face. But he forced himself to be content with the thought: one, day, Jose, I'll get even with you. I swear it on Martha's grave.

The wedding ceremony was due to take place on a rostrum which had been erected in the centre of the open space between the tents.

'We stand up here,' said Pedro, taking his position. Rand joined him.

The crowd, which had been excitedly

chattering away, fell into a hushed silence. All eyes were on a tent about a hundred yards away to the left. Rand found that he too was staring in that direction.

The silence grew longer. Perhaps Alicia had changed her mind, thought Rand. It would be ironical if it were she, and not him, who called off the wedding. Here he was, probably the most unwilling bridegroom to get married in Mexico and maybe the bride would be the one who failed to turn up at the wedding.

His hopes were dashed when a white figure appeared from the tent. She began to move slowly towards the rostrum. Rand had half-expected that there would be some smiles at the sight of this woman with the disfigured face dressed up for her weddingday, but to his relief there was no such reaction. Instead there was clapping as she passed down the row of tents. It was an unexpected reaction and to Rand it showed the warmth of feeling and generosity of the women who were greeting Alicia in this way.

Rand glanced sideways at Jose. There was a scowl on the bandit's face. It was obvious that he had been surprised by the reaction. It gave Rand a moment of satisfaction as he realized that Jose had been beaten, even if only in a minor way.

As Alicia came nearer Rand realized something else. She was wearing a wedding-dress with a thick veil that completely hid her face. She came slowly up to the rostrum as though savouring every moment. She stopped at the foot of the platform and Rand helped her up.

Rand glanced at her, trying to gauge her expression, but the veil effectively hid her face. Mendez took up his place in front of them.

He started asking the time-honoured questions:

'Do you, Clive Rand, take this woman, Alicia Lorez as your wife?'

There was a pause. Rand knew that a multitude of eyes were on him. His mind went back to the time when he had married

Martha. It had been in a small church in a small town in Texas named Summerfields. There had only been a couple of dozen or so in the congregation. Just his parents, Martha's parents and a few friends of the families. It had been the happiest day of his life. Now somehow he felt that he was deserting Martha and desecrating her memory by going through this sham of a wedding.

Why not say he wasn't going to go through with it? Jose would have him shot, but what did it matter? Part of him had already died when Martha died. If it wasn't for the fact that Alicia would be shot with him, he would go ahead with the idea. There was also one other consideration. He would like to stay alive to get even with Jose. He wanted to see the fear in Jose's eyes when eventually they came face to face on even terms. He wanted to see Jose die to satisfy the burning hatred which was inside him.

'Well?' asked Mendez, anxiously.

'I do,' said Rand. There was a gasp of relief from the crowd.

CHAPTER 8

The fiesta was in full swing. The tequila was flowing freely. The wedding service had been over in a matter of minutes. After Rand had signified his acceptance of the bride, Alicia had declared her acceptance of him as her husband. She had lifted the heavy veil from her face to speak her words. He had glanced at her to see what was her reaction to the farce. Her face was drawn and he thought he spotted the hint of a tear in her eye. It added to Rand's determination to get even with Jose when the time came.

After Mendez had declared them man and wife, the crowd had waited expectantly for Rand to kiss the bride. Alicia's veil was still raised and Rand kissed her perfunctorily on the lips. However his bride was determined that it would be a meaningful kiss and she clung to him for several long moments. When she broke away her veil descended like the curtain at the end of a play.

Was it the end though? Rand wondered several times during the next few hours as the tempo of the fiesta gathered pace. The rostrum which had been used for their marriage was now the centre of activity as dancers came and went – the women invariably in colourful swirling skirts. Several of the musicians took their places on the stage to perform their party-pieces. One violinist in particular was a virtuoso and received well-deserved applause. The master of ceremonies, a big man who wore a colourful army uniform, announced each participant in a loud voice. Several of the men who appeared on the stage sang sad songs. Most of the songs were sung with heartfelt sadness about the loss of a loved one, or regret at leaving their homeland. There were tears in the eyes of many of the audience as they listened to the artistes' renderings.

Mendez had seated himself next to Rand

and had assumed the duty of guardian, supplying Rand with food from time to time and offering him tequila, which Rand refused, not because he disapproved of the drink, but because he guessed it would give him a terrible head in the morning.

He turned his thoughts to Alicia. She had promised that she would not expect him to treat the marriage as a genuine one. But what if, in the anticipation of the wedding and the excitement of the fiesta, she had changed her mind? After all, it was a fair assumption that this would be Alicia's only chance of getting married in the camp. He had noticed one thing while he had been sitting watching the fiesta: there were at a rough guess about twice as many women as men in the camp. Many of the women were quite attractive. Some of them would disappear from time to time into one of the tents with a man. He would guess that the women were not inviting the men into their tents to show them their butterfly collection. The whole scenario suggested that

Alicia's chance of finding a husband would have virtually disappeared given the surplus of women over men. All of which could add to a worrying situation for him. Perhaps he should have some of that tequila after all.

He nodded to Mendez when he next proffered him the bottle. Mendez grinned to show his approval. He had begun to get worried about the American. There was something wrong with a man who didn't have a drink on his wedding-night. But now Rand had restored his faith in mankind.

'By the way,' asked Rand, as he gingerly tasted the tequila, 'where is Alicia?'

'I expect she's getting the marriage-bed ready,' smirked Mendez.

'This isn't going to be real marriage in the true sense of the word,' said Rand, as he took another pull at the tequila. To his surprise he discovered that it was quite pleasant to drink. 'This is a marriage of convenience. It has been arranged by Jose for his convenience,' he concluded bitterly.

'Don't worry, *amigo*,' said Mendez, waving

the bottle of tequila in the air to emphasize his point. 'As you Americans say, "in the dark all women look the same".' He further emphasized the point by collapsing in a drunken stupor. In fact Rand had wondered why he hadn't collapsed earlier.

He asked one of the Mexicans seated nearby which was Mendez's tent. He was directed to one slightly further away than Alicia's. Rand picked him up and carried him to his tent. On the way he had to pass Jose who was seated on his usual chair.

'Hey, *señor*,' Jose greeted him as he passed. 'It won't be long now till your wedding-night starts.' All those who were gathered around Jose roared with laughter.

Rand deposited Mendez in his tent. He was about to take the half-empty bottle of tequila back with him when he changed his mind and left it by Mendez's side. Something told Rand that he might need a clear head tonight after all.

Instead of rejoining the fiesta, Rand made his way to Alicia's tent. To his relief it was empty. He lay down on the bed with the intention of trying to clarify his thoughts about exactly how he would deal with his wife when she came to the tent. The more he thought about it the more her passionate kiss told him that she would expect him to fulfil his marital duty. Then what could happen if he refused her demands? They say that hell hath no fury like a woman scorned. In that case half a dozen hells would have no fury like a wife who was scorned. His guess would be that she would take her complaint to Jose. The bandit-in-chief, seeing that his attempt to find an amicable solution to Rand's unwelcome presence in the camp had been scuppered by Rand, would argue that it left him with only one alternative. He, Rand would have to die.

CHAPTER 9

Rand was lying on his bed – or rather Alicia's bed, he corrected himself. Outside he could still hear the sounds of the fiesta. It had now obviously developed into a drunken orgy. Women were running around, shrieking with laughter or screaming. Men were obviously running after them, shouting for them to stop. One woman came into the tent by mistake, then seeing Rand lying on the bed made her apologises in confusion and left hurriedly.

Anger boiled inside Rand that he should be a party to such debauchery that he had been used as an excuse to start the whole sorry state of affairs. Of course it suited Jose to have a ready-made excuse like the wedding to allow everyone to let off steam. Life up here in the mountain must be monotonous and soul-destroying. Any chance of adding a little variety to the bandits' way of life would be seized upon avidly. And of course, he, Rand, had provided the ideal excuse. In terms of variety and excitement the wedding had probably provided enough of those ingredients to last for the next three months. He himself was an army officer, and he knew how important it was to maintain the men's morale at times of boredom. Yes, Jose must have thought that it had been manna from heaven when Rand had given him this opportunity for an orgy.

The sounds of the musicians had died away some time before. Rand could see through the partly open flap in the tent that darkness had fallen. He wondered when Alicia would appear to claim her marriage dues. Well, there was no way that he was going to allow the farce to continue in that direction. He would tell her that they would be husband and wife in name only – until he had a chance to escape from this place. She had agreed to the arrangement originally and that was how it was going to be.

Suddenly the flap of the tent burst open. For a fleeting second Rand thought that Alicia had had enough of waiting and had rushed into the tent. Then he realized that the newcomer was a drunken Mexican. Rand seized him by the seat of his pants and hurled him into the darkness. The man's cry of pain gave Rand some slight satisfaction.

It was probably an hour or so later when Alicia finally appeared. By then the camp had gone strangely quiet. In fact it was almost uncanny the way the noise and activity had suddenly declined. Rand guessed that nearly all the bandits were by then too drunk to take part in any more physical action. They were probably all in a drunken stupor.

Alicia opened the flap of the tent and stood there. It was too dark for Rand to distinguish the expression on her face.

'If you want to get away from the camp,' she whispered, 'now is your chance.'

'How? Why?' stammered Rand.

'Because you don't want to stay here for the rest of your life, do you?' she whispered.

'No,' agreed Rand, with no lack of determination.

'Right, let's go,' she said.

'How?' Rand was still puzzled.

'I've got two horses waiting. Be quiet as you follow me. Everyone is asleep, but there's still the chance that someone will see us.'

She led the way between the tents. There were bodies here and there lying outside the tents. Most of them were men's, the women obviously having chosen the warmth of the tents after their orgy. Occasionally a man stirred in his sleep as they went silently past. On one occasion Rand stopped in his tracks as a bandit showed every sign of coming to life. The man groaned a couple of times, uttered the name 'Carmen' then, to Rand's relief, went back to sleep again.

Alicia waited impatiently for him to catch her up. He followed her to where two mountain ponies were tethered to a solitary tree. She unhitched them and passed the reins of one to him. They were small horses and when Rand mounted his feet almost touched the ground.

'Let's go,' said Alicia, urgently.

She led the way. Rand saw from the position of the stars that they were heading south – towards Limos, he guessed. However it wasn't the stars but the moon that was important. Without its guiding light they would not be able to see where they were going. They rode in single file with Rand obediently following Alicia. With the passing of the minutes Rand's heart lightened. He was getting away from Jose, he told himself. Every few hundred yards that they put between themselves and the bandit and his men were vitally important. Rand knew that Jose would not be able to mount a search party until the morning. Jose would assume that he and Alicia were still in their tent. By the time he discovered the truth they would be almost in Limos and there would be nothing the bandit could do about it.

Rand knew that he would be eternally grateful to Alicia for helping him to escape. Of course, not grateful enough to allow her to adopt her full duties as a wife, but surely there would be some other way in which he could show his appreciation. There was a bank in Limos; he could arrange to have money transferred to it and so reward her financially. Yes, that sounded like a reasonable idea.

Rand guessed they had been riding for about an hour by then. Progress had of necessity been slow. They had ridden in single file because the paths were narrow, and there was no room for them to ride two abreast. Apart from seeing that he kept a reasonable distance behind Alicia, Rand also kept a constant watch on the moon. When they had started out the sky had been reasonably cloudless but lately the cloud had started to build up from the west. Stay clear for the rest of the night, pleaded Rand as he watched the progress of the clouds with anxious eyes.

The horses picked their way gingerly along the mountain path. How far had they come from the camp? Three miles? Five miles? Riding along this rough terrain made it difficult to judge how far they had come. One thing was certain, though. They had not put enough distance between themselves and the camp for them to be reasonably content with their progress.

A few minutes later the moon was about to slip behind one of the dark clouds. In itself that might not be too serious, but there was a bank of dark clouds behind it. Rand knew that at least for some time they would have to pull up.

Alicia confirmed this by reining in her pony. She turned in her saddle.

'We'll have to stay here until the moon comes out again,' she stated.

CHAPTER 10

Jose, who had been an army captain in the Civil War, possessed the soldier's knack of knowing when danger threatened, or at least when things weren't as they should be. He awoke just before dawn with a huge hangover, which was only to be expected after the excesses of the night before, and the uneasy feeling that something was wrong. He kicked one of his lieutenants, Fernando, awake.

'Go and see if the gringo is in his tent,' he commanded.

'What if he is making love to Alicia?' demanded Fernando.

'He'll probably be glad of the interruption,' snapped Jose. 'Now get going.'

His lieutenant was back in five minutes with the news that neither Rand nor Alicia were in the tent and that it didn't appear as though they had slept in the bed. Also the two horses which had been tethered near the edge of the camp had disappeared. Jose's face blackened with anger.

'Who was supposed to guard the tent last night?'

'Tomos,' said a relieved Fernando. After all, it could have been him.

'Fetch him,' commanded Jose. While he was waiting for his return he gave the order to another of his lieutenants to fetch the Apache Indian, Snow on the Grass. Fernando arrived first with a terrified Tomos.

'Where were you last night when you were supposed to be watching the American and Alicia?' demanded Jose, icily.

'I – I went to Bianca's tent,' stammered Tomos. He went down on his knees, shutting his eyes. 'Please forgive me. It won't happen again.'

'You've never said a truer word,' said Jose, as he shot Tomos between the eyes. 'Get him away from here,' he said kicking the corpse in the ribs.

The Apache Indian arrived.

'I want you to trail two people who left the camp last night. A man and a woman. They were on horseback. They would probably have headed for Limos.'

The Apache did not reply. He rarely wasted energy by talking.

In ten minutes the search-party had gathered. There was Jose himself, three of Jose's lieutenants and the Apache. They set off on horseback following the trail that Rand and Alicia had taken the night before.

By now the sun had risen. The party moved slowly, the Indian with his eyes glued to the trail. Now and again he would jump from his horse to examine a particular mark on the ground.

'Can't we go any faster?' demanded Jose after one of these stops.

'See that.' The Indian pointed to a barely distinguishable trail to the left. 'They could have gone that way. If you want to catch them I must make sure.'

After that Jose left the Apache to his own devices. The sun rose higher and several of the search-party began to mop their brows.

'If we don't catch up with them soon, they'll be half-way to Limos,' said a disgruntled Jose.

'If we catch them then we can still bring them back,' said a hopeful Fernando.

'The nearer we get to Limos what will we find?' demanded Jose.

'Some mountain streams,' ventured Fernando.

'Alphonso's men, you idiot,' snapped Jose. 'It's their territory, and they'll be guarding it.'

A short time later the Apache gave what was for him a shout of triumph, but to the others seemed more like a grunt.

'They stopped here for the night.' He pointed at a worn patch on the path.

'The moon must have disappeared,' said a thoughtful Jose.

'The man slept here,' the Apache pointed

to a flattened area. 'And the woman slept here.' He pointed to a spot about three yards away.

'The American still isn't making love to the beautiful Alicia,' Jose announced to the rest of the party. They roared with laughter, partly at the joke but most at the fact that Jose seemed in a good humour once again.

About a mile further on the Apache jumped down from his horse once again.

'What is it?' demanded Jose.

'One of the horses is lame,' announced the Indian. 'The American is walking while the lady is riding the other horse.'

'Where's the lame horse?' demanded Jose.

His question was answered when they rounded the next bend. The horse was peacefully grazing by the side of the trail.

CHAPTER 11

At the first sign of the sky lightening Rand awoke and glanced at Alicia. She was laying curled up a few feet away from him.

'Wake up,' he said.

She grumbled as she gained consciousness. Then, realizing that they could now start on their journey once again, she hurriedly rolled up her blanket.

In two minutes they were on their way.

'I wonder how long it will take Jose to realize we are missing?' asked Alicia, as they took up their usual position on the trail with her pony in front.

'We'll have to wait and see,' Rand supplied.

The sun rose above the horizon. They were making steady if not spectacular progress when the accident happened. Alicia's pony stumbled. Before she could regain control of him he was down on his knees.

She jumped off.

'What's the matter with him?' she demanded, as she tried to drag him back to his feet.

'He's sprained a fetlock,' announced Rand, after examining him.

'What does that mean?'

'It means you won't be able to ride him any more.'

'But I'll never get to Limos without a pony,' she wailed.

'You can have mine,' stated Rand.

'Thanks.' She jumped at the idea. 'But what will you do?' she demanded, after reconsidering the offer.

'I'll take the scenic route.' Rand gazed at the mountains which stretched above them.

'I don't like to leave you here without a horse,' she half-protested.

'I'll be all right. My ankle seems to have healed. I'm used to walking in the mountains.'

'I'll be on my way then,' she smiled at him. 'And thanks for letting me have your horse.'

'Don't mention it. You'd better hurry. Jose can't be too far behind.'

She hesitated.

'He'd have better horses than these. I suppose he could catch me up.'

'It's a possibility,' agreed Rand.

'Isn't there some other way we could go on together?' She was less sure of herself now.

'I'll walk behind you. Perhaps we can put another couple of miles behind us before Jose arrives on the scene.'

They set off with Rand walking behind. Progress was rather slower than before. Alicia turned round a few times to gauge Rand's progress.

'Can't you go any faster?' she eventually demanded.

'I think we'd better revert to the earlier plan,' said Rand. 'You go on ahead.'

'But what if my horse breaks down? They were two old nags which had been left out in the field. This one could easily stumble and fall also.'

'You've got a point there,' said Rand, stroking his recently sprouted beard.

'Well, don't just stand there saying "you've got a point there",' she flared up. 'Think of something.'

'There's only one thing we can do,' said Rand.

'What's that?' she demanded, hopefully.

'We'll have to go up into the mountains.' He pointed up to where the mountains rose a further 3,000 feet above the path they had been following.

'What good will that do? Apart from giving us a good view of Jose and his bandits?'

'In the first place it will give us time. And in the second place it will give us the advantage if we must take on Jose in a fight.'

She looked up and down the trail, undecided.

'How can you talk about taking on Jose and his men?' she demanded. 'We haven't got a gun?'

'Never mind about that now. Are you

coming up into the mountains with me?'

She took one last longing glance at the trail ahead. She turned to him.

'I haven't got much choice, have I?' she conceded.

'Right. Let's go,' said Rand, briskly.

She had expected him to turn off the trail and start heading up the mountain from where they were standing. Instead Rand carried on along the trail.

'I thought we were going up into the mountains,' she protested.

'We've got to find the right place to turn off,' Rand explained. 'Jose will have brought a tracker with him–'

'The Apache Indian,' she interrupted.

'Exactly. So we've to try and make his job as hard as possible by turning off the trail at a point where it will be difficult for him to pick up our tracks. Here, for instance.'

They had reached a long ridge of granite where the path had become a narrow ledge along its length. To their left the granite rose gradually for a couple of hundred feet before being replaced by shale. Rand turned towards the mountain leading Alicia's horse. They moved up slowly, the horse being an unwilling accomplice. However, in the end they managed to climb the granite ridge.

'The Indian will find it hard to find out where we left the trail,' said Rand, as they surveyed the scenery below.

'How much further up will we have to go?' asked Alicia, as she turned and gazed upwards.

'Oh, I don't know. A thousand feet, I expect,' supplied Rand.

'All right. Let's get on with it,' snapped Alicia.

They had climbed a few hundred feet when Rand whispered:

'Get down.' He suited his own action to the words by diving behind a rock and pulling the pony after him. Alicia jumped behind an adjoining rock.

On the trail below Jose and his men were clearly visible. Rand counted three men, plus Jose and the Indian. That made five he would be up against if it ever came to battle. He watched them as they moved slowly along the trail, with the Indian leading.

'How long do you think it will take them to realize we're up here?' whispered Alicia, who had moved closer to Rand.

'Long enough, I hope,' he answered enigmatically. He watched as the search-party disappeared round a bend. The Indian had already passed the spot where they had turned off. 'Right, let's go,' said Rand. He pulled the pony from its hiding-place and started leading the way upwards again.

As they climbed higher the wind gained in strength. Rand glanced at Alicia. She was wearing a thin dress and the cloak over it and very little else, he guessed. He took off his jacket and handed it to her.

'I'm all right, thank you,' she said, through chattering teeth.

'Put it on,' commanded Rand, 'we don't want you suffering from the cold.'

She accepted the jacket with bad grace.

'I should have gone ahead on my own,' she

stated. 'I would be half-way to Limos by now.'

'Maybe,' said Rand laconically.

'What do you mean "maybe",' she snapped as she turned on him. 'I shouldn't have listened to you. I should have stayed down on the path.'

Rand thought about pointing out that it had been her choice, but wisely decided against it. It was obvious that she was in a disagreeable mood. A very disagreeable mood, he reflected as they pushed ahead.

Rand was saved from being further harangued by Alicia when they came upon a path. It was probably 1,000 feet above the path they had just left, but seemed to be going in the same direction.

'We're in luck,' Alicia observed.

'I knew it was there all the time,' said Rand.

'Huh, very funny,' she said, grumpily. But not too grumpily, Rand noted.

They had been travelling along the path for about a quarter of an hour, with Alicia on the pony, when she turned to Rand.

'I'm sorry I was rude to you back there. It's just that I'm cold and hungry. I don't suppose you've got any food?'

'Sorry,' said Rand.

They moved steadily along the path. There was no sign of the path below, which the bandits would probably be following, unless the Indian had realized his mistake by now and had turned back and started to climb the mountain after them. In order to check that possibility Rand kept turning back from time to time to ascertain that the path behind was clear. Alicia could not see his concern since she was keeping her full concentration on seeing that her pony did not slip, for which he was thankful.

The other thing of concern to Rand was that the path seemed to be sloping downwards. At first it was merely an impression, but as they moved further along the impression grew into a conviction. He glanced ahead at Alicia, but she was carrying on along the trail seemingly blissfully unaware of where the path was leading.

They rounded a bend and now the path began to descend steeply.

'We're going down,' Alicia announced, seemingly unconcerned.

There was no doubt about it, the path was descending, and if Rand was receiving his regular payments from the army he would have put his monthly wages on the fact that the path would soon join the one that they had left, below. Then what would happen?

He was saved from further conjecture by the fact that when they rounded the next bend two of Jose's men were standing there with drawn pistols.

'We meet again, *señor*,' said one, whose name, Rand remembered, was Calvero.

CHAPTER 12

Rand knew that he was as near to death as he had ever been in his encounters in the army with the enemy. Paco and his companion were covering Rand and Alicia with their pistols.

'I know that Jose would like to have the pleasure of shooting you himself,' said Paco. 'But if you make one false move I will have pleasure in doing the task for him.'

The four were like statues on the path, with Alicia still seated on her horse. Paco gestured for Alicia to dismount. Rand had realized that the one thing in his favour was the fact that the path was too narrow for two people to stand side by side. He was therefore partly obscured by Alicia as she slipped off her horse. In that split second Rand took the penknife out of his trouser-pocket and opened it. It had last been used in the making of a whistle for the young boy back in the camp. But Rand knew that it had a deadly blade which he regularly sharpened on one of the camp's guns.

Paco took the horse's reins from Alicia and drew the horse behind him so that the four were now lined up on the path. For a moment Rand read indecision on Paco's face. Rand felt sure that if Jose were here he would instantly know what to do with his two captives on this narrow path. But the situation was unfamiliar to Paco and therefore he hesitated. It gave Rand newfound hope. An indecisive opponent was an opponent at a disadvantage and Rand hoped that he would be able to exploit that indecision when Paco made his move.

'Calvero – take care of her,' said Paco, indicating to his companion that Alicia would be his responsibility from now on. 'And treat her carefully,' he added. 'Jose has his own plans for her.'

Calvero gestured with his gun that Alicia

should join him. She glanced appealingly at Rand, who gave nothing away with his stony face. Her shoulders slumped in resignation as she realized that Rand was not going to be of any help to her. The pair moved a short distance along the path, leaving Paco to deal with Rand.

The Mexican had now obviously made up his mind what to do with Rand. He approached him.

'Turn round,' he said.

By making the request Paco had shown his intention. He was going to club him on the head. It meant that for a couple of seconds Paco's gun would not be pointing at him since he would have to reverse the gun in his hand. If Rand could use those couple of seconds to his advantage he might yet be able to turn the tables on the Mexicans. Rand glanced at Calvero who had moved even further along the path. He must now be at least fifty feet away, Rand concluded.

'Hurry up, we haven't got all day,' snapped Paco.

Rand shrugged. It was an expressive shrug. The sort of shrug which suggested that there was nothing Rand could do but comply with the demands of the man with the gun. Rand turned slowly.

Paco was about three paces behind him. Rand knew that he had to time it to perfection. One split second of error and Paco would dispatch him to oblivion with a blow on the head. Then it would only be a matter of time before Jose delivered the final bullet. Rand's one advantage was that he felt completely calm. He knew that it was an attribute which had helped him at periods of danger in the past. He only hoped that his experience in the past would hold good now.

Rand watched Paco's shadow on the granite wall to his right as the Mexican approached him. Paco moved slowly, as though sensing that there might be some danger in what was apparently a straight-forward way of dispatching his opponent. Step up behind him, hit him on the head, then, hey-presto – one less troublesome enemy to deal with!

Paco was now the required distance behind Rand. He reversed the revolver in his hand, raised it to deliver the blow – but before it came Rand swung round with lightning speed for a big man and stabbed Paco in the heart. In one movement Rand grabbed Paco's gun and aimed at Calvero who was standing stock-still, as though mesmerized by the sudden turn in events. In that second Rand shot Calvero in the heart. He watched as Calvero slowly slid off the path and began an ungainly descent down the mountainside.

'You were great! You did it! You were marvellous!' yelled an excited Alicia as she rushed towards him.

CHAPTER 13

The rest of their journey to Limos was largely uneventful. About a hundred yards further along the path where they had been confronted by Paco and Calvero they came across the Mexicans' horses tied to a tree. They mounted them and set off for Limos.

Alicia was clearly still excited by Rand's success.

'You were fantastic,' she enthused. 'The way you stabbed Paco in the heart without being able to see what you were doing.'

'I could see his shadow,' explained Rand.

'And then to shoot Calvero with one shot.'

'I've won medals for shooting,' said Rand. 'And now if you don't mind I'd rather not talk about it.'

'Oh, all right,' said Alicia, rather peeved by his response.

Most of the rest of the journey was conducted in silence. They did have one break – to take advantage of the fact that both horses carried some food in the saddlebags. When Rand had judged that they had put sufficient distance between themselves and the bandits he called a halt.

'I shouldn't think there's any danger of Jose following us now,' he stated.

'Not if they realize how you managed to dispatch Calvero and Paco,' agreed Alicia.

'They'll probably have found the two bodies by now,' stated Rand. 'They'll realize one thing for sure.'

'What's that?' demanded Alicia, as she munched an apple.

'That I've got their two guns,' stated Rand.

'And when they see how you killed Calvero at that distance with one shot to the heart...' she glanced at Rand and saw the look of disapproval on his face. She held up her hands in mock surrender. 'All right, I promise I won't mention it again.'

They were soon on their way again. Rand noted with interest that the terrain was changing. They were leaving the mountains behind them. They were soon riding along the plain where their progress was quicker. They even met a few *vaqueros*, some of them in charge of a handful of cattle. The Mexicans invariably regarded them with interest, especially the *señorita* before wishing them *'buenos dias'*.

It was late in the afternoon when Rand spotted a town in the distance.

'Limos?' he asked.

'Yes,' Alicia confirmed.

'Where do you intend staying?'

'My brother Chris lives here. He's a sergeant in the army. What about you? What are you going to do now?'

'I'll find somewhere to stay tonight. Then tomorrow I'll call to see the mayor.'

'Alphonso.'

'Yes. I'll tell him where Jose's camp is situated. After that it's up to him whether he wants to go after him or not.'

'You wouldn't go back up to the camp yourself, would you?'

There was concern in her voice. It was nice to know that somebody was worried about his well-being. Even though it was a Mexican whom he would never see again.

'You forget, I'm a map-maker. I'll draw him a map of the mountains and the route we used. After that it's up to him.'

'That's all right then.' She smiled.

Her face really lit up when she smiled. If it were not for that disfiguring scar she would be a beautiful young woman.

She caught him staring at her.

'What is it?' she asked with concern.

'I don't know. Sometimes saying goodbye can be very hard.'

'I know.' She stared at him with large brown eyes.

'We've had a few adventures, haven't we?'

'You can say that again.'

'I saw you kill two men.'

'I don't wasn't to hear that again.'

'You're a strange one.' She examined him

with her head to one side. 'If you were a Mexican you'd be boasting about it for years.'

'I think we'd better be saying goodbye.' He held out his hand.

She ignored it. Moving close to him she kissed him on the lips. The kiss went on until at last he broke away.

'That's so that you'll remember me,' she stated, before turning and walking away.

CHAPTER 14

Rand did think about her during the next few months. Partly because his daily existence in the army camp was dull and boring and he missed the excitement of the time they had spent together. His duties consisted of helping to train new recruits. These came in various forms and from a variety of backgrounds. Their ages, too, varied from eighteen to forty. Some were what his sergeant labelled riff-raff; others had had some kind of education, and would have been more suitable in an office job. All had one thing in common – they wanted to escape from their way of life as civilians, and saw in the army the ideal opportunity to do so.

They were soon disillusioned.

'I always give them one month,' said the sergeant, an Irishman named O'Rourke. He was right. However when they became disillusioned with army life they were forced to face up to the fact that they were trapped for two years – the standard signing-on period. And unless they could find $1,000 they couldn't buy their way out of the predicament in which they found themselves.

Another of O'Rourke's dictums was:

'Half of them will be on laudanum, before they finish their two years.' Once again he was unfortunately right. The number of cases of laudanum users in the camp increased almost daily. It became a serious problem. It undermined authority and spread insubordination and discontent like a plague. One result was there were often more recruits in the jail than there were on parade. When Rand was summoned to the colonel's office, he guessed it had something to do with the drug menace. He was right.

'Sit down, Lieutenant,' said Colonel Stanton. When Rand was seated the commanding officer continued: 'I won't beat about the bush. I want your assistance in helping to crush this drug menace which is undermining every section of this camp's activity.'

Rand remained silent. He didn't see that he could do much about it. The military police had tried to cut off the supply of drugs to the camp by cancelling all visits to the nearest town, Hawkesville. But the men were still getting their supply of drugs. A favourite ruse was to apply for compassionate leave, saying that one of their relatives had died. The colonel couldn't refuse such a request. When the soldier returned the chances were that he would be carrying drugs which he would proceed to distribute to his companions. These thoughts flashed through Rand's mind as he waited for the colonel to come to the reason for this interview.

'I have a dangerous mission for you,' said the colonel, clearing his throat. 'Firstly, I must emphasize that because of the danger involved, you are not obliged to accept it. It will not count against you for any future chance of promotion.'

Rand again waited while the colonel glanced at the top sheet of a pile of papers on his desk.

'I have a transcript here,' he tapped the paper, 'of the report from the mayor of Limos. He said he was very impressed with your survey of the prospective railway from San Caldiz to Limos.'

'It was a … challenging assignment,' Rand stated.

The colonel turned the sheet over to read the next one. 'It says in the report you wrote for me when you returned from the assignment that you were captured by outlaws, but managed to escape.' The colonel turned his attention again to the report. 'It doesn't exactly say how you *did* manage to escape.'

'I had help from a young lady,' Rand admitted.

The colonel stared at him thoughtfully. Eventually he turned his attention back to the report.

'It says here that the leader of the outlaws is a man named Jose del Monte.'

'That's right. He was the outlaws' leader.'

'Our information is that he is the person responsible for bringing the opium over the border from Mexico. In the first place he brings it from the poppy-fields which lie to the south of Limos. He brings it along mountain tracks which aren't shown on any maps – mostly because the Mexicans don't have any maps.' The colonel permitted himself a smile.

'What exactly do you want me to do, sir?' asked Rand.

'It's entirely up to you. You are requested by the mayor of Limos to attend the ceremony of the cutting of the first sod to start building the railway. This is really a cover for you to help to lead Alphonso and his men to the camp where Jose del Monte is hiding. You can take your time in coming to a decision.'

'I'll take the assignment,' Rand told a rather surprised Colonel Stanton.

CHAPTER 15

The ceremony to celebrate that work on the railway line from Limos to San Caldiz was about to start was held in the open. Those present consisted of a motley collection of dignitaries, several representatives of the armed forces, and the general public. As far as Rand could tell he was the only American representative.

Alphonso was the central character. He was seated on a rather grand chair which had been bedecked with ribbons. The chair was situated on a small makeshift stage. The stage was not large enough to hold another chair. This meant that Alphonso was secure in his status as the most important person in Limos.

Several other of the town's dignitaries were seated in front of the stage. Rand himself had been offered one of the chairs, but had politely refused. Instead he had taken up a position standing at the back. Because of his height he had no difficulty in seeing the whole of the proceedings. The only disadvantage he could find in his present position was that he was in close proximity to the band. The moment they started playing he guessed he would be subjected to an ear-splitting cacophony of sound. He was right. When the band did start playing it was obvious that what they lacked in musical technique they tried to make up for in excessive volume.

Fortunately the band's performance proved to be short, since they soon had to make way for the star of the show – Alphonso. He was sporting a major's army uniform. Rand conceded that it was possible Alphonso had been a major in the Mexican army, but he was sceptical about the row of medals which Alphonso was wearing. If he had really been involved in so many battles, he must have spent the whole of the Civil War riding flat out from one battle scene to another. He probably had a medal from the battle of Alamo, although he would only have been about ten years old at the time. Rand smiled at the thought.

Alphonso's speech was obviously going to go on for some time. Rand glanced idly at the ordinary inhabitants of Limos who were gathered on a slight rise, from which position they had an excellent view of the proceedings. He discovered that he was searching for a certain face: Alicia's. He had thought of her several times during the past six months, wondering what had become of her. In fact he had drawn several pictures of her. He was a good artist and often occupied his spare time in the army camp in drawing some particular scene or person. He had drawn Alicia's face from memory and although he wasn't too happy with the results, it had helped to confirm what he had already assumed – that she had excellent bone-structure. If it hadn't been for her scarred skin she would have been a very beautiful young woman.

He searched for her among the crowd, but without success. Alphonso's speech showed no sign of coming to an end. Rand's thoughts again turned to the time he had spent in the outlaws' camp up in the mountains. He had gone through the farce of a wedding ceremony with Alicia. But was it a farce? She had said she would never hold him to it, but maybe, in the eyes of the church, they were officially married. True, he had submitted to the ceremony under duress. True, also, he wasn't a Roman Catholic, but what was the legal position about the marriage? His wife, Martha, had been a Roman Catholic. It had always been a source of regret to her, that he had never embraced the Catholic faith. His religious convictions were almost non-existent. The only concession he had granted her was that if they had children then they could be brought up in the Roman Catholic faith. Unfortunately they had never been blessed with children.

His thoughts were interrupted by the evident signs that Alphonso's speech was coming to an end. Rand's gaze again wandered around the crowd of onlookers. He thought he caught a glint of steel from someone near a wall. His impression was confirmed when there was the unmistakable sound of a rifle shot. It was followed by the sight of Alphonso instinctively clutching the red stain which was slowly spreading over his medals.

CHAPTER 16

Half an hour later Rand was seated in Alphonso's office. Or rather, the late Alphonso's office, he mentally corrected himself. Seated in the chair which Alphonso would have been occupying was the Captain of Police, Perez.

'It's difficult to know where to begin,' said Perez, spreading his hands in a gesture of uncertainty.

He was a young man, probably about his own age, Rand guessed. At the moment he looked as though he had all the troubles of the world on his shoulders.

'Alphonso sent for me to try to break up the supply of opium to the outlaws. I expect this plan has now gone by the board,' explained Rand.

'I should think that is so. My main

concern at the moment is to find the person who killed Alphonso. That's what the public would expect.'

'I think I know him,' stated Rand.

'You do?' Perez's voice rose in surprise.

'I caught a glimpse of him before he fired the shot. He was standing by the wall.'

'What's his name?' demanded Perez, excitedly.

'Fernando. I met him when I was kidnapped by Jose and his men.'

'Yes. I heard about that. Well, at least I've got a name. That should go some way towards getting the politicians off my back.'

Perez did seem more relaxed, Rand could see. Aloud he said:

'Well, I'll be on my way back over the border.'

'You're not staying for Alphonso's funeral?'

'I hardly knew him. I only met him a couple of times. He seemed a nice guy.'

'Yes. Well, we'll have to appoint a new mayor. We're too small a town to have a deputy. When one is appointed maybe he'll get in touch with you to put the plan to catch the opium-dealers back on the road.'

Rand stood up. He shook hands with the captain. He was about to leave the office when he was struck by a thought.

'I could give you a picture of Fernando.'

'You've got one of the new inventions? A...' he struggled for the word.

'A camera?' Rand smiled. 'No, I could draw his face.'

'You're an artist?' Perez became excited again.

'Not exactly. But I drew the plans for the railway.'

'It would certainly help if you could draw Fernando.'

Rand thought for a few moments.

'It means I'll have to stay here today. It would be better if I drew a dozen or so pictures for you. You could put them up at suitable places in the town.'

'It would be great. We have a hotel in the town. I'll arrange for you to stay there. Of course, all your expenses will be paid for by the town.'

'Thanks.'

'When will you be ready to start?'

'Straight away,' Rand told a rather surprised Perez.

Rand was ushered into a small room. It had a desk and a window which provided him with enough light for his self-appointed task. Perez himself brought in the supply of paper and pens.

'If you need anything else, just let me know. I'll be in the office at the end of the corridor for the rest of the day. I've got to face a number of politicians, but at least I'll be able to tell them that something is being done.'

Rand smiled.

'There is one other thing before I start the drawings.'

'What's that?'

'I assume you want to offer a reward for Fernando's recapture?'

'Naturally.'

'How much do you want me to put on the poster?'

Perez thought for a moment. Finally he announced:

'A thousand American dollars.'

Rand set about his task. From time to time he glanced up at the window to check that the light would be sufficient for him to keep on producing his posters. From time to time, too, Perez came in to see how he was progressing.

When Rand showed him his first poster Perez was delighted with it.

'It's great. It's fabulous,' he enthused.

Rand smiled at his reaction. 'I think I've captured his face.'

The day dragged on and Rand produced another half a dozen drawings. As light began to fade he took them into Perez's office.

'I'm afraid I can't do any more today. The daylight is going. It'll soon be too dark for me to see what I'm doing.'

Perez accepted the posters.

'They're great. They're all great,' he said, checking through them. 'I've arranged for you to stay in the Ritz Hotel,' he added. 'It's not as posh as it sounds. But it's clean. And the food is good.'

Having promised to return in the morning, Rand set off for the Ritz Hotel. In the gathering dusk he could see that from the outside, the hotel had little to recommend it. It needed repainting, it had several cracked windows which needed replacing, and even the verandas outside some of the bedroom windows looked as though they might collapse if someone stepped out on them.

Inside however, Rand's impression changed. When he announced his name, the buxom white-haired lady behind the desk greeted him with a welcoming smile.

'Captain Perez said you would be coming.'

He was shown up to his room by a youth. The room was large and when Rand tried the bed, he found that it was quite comfortable.

'If there is anything you want, let me know,' the youth said, having deftly caught the coin which Rand had tossed to him.

The food, too, Rand discovered, was excellent. Having washed down the best steak he had had for ages with half a bottle of excellent wine, he was preparing to retire to bed when a familiar figure burst into the dining-room.

'Alicia,' he exclaimed. 'It's great to see you again.'

It was soon obvious that his enthusiasm didn't seem to be shared by her. Her face didn't wear the expected welcoming smile. In fact when he studied her face by the light of the oil-lamp he saw that it wore a distinctly worried expression.

'You must leave town, at once,' she stated.

'What's the hurry? Anyhow, I've got a task to finish tomorrow.'

She sat down on the chair opposite him. Her eyes shone by the flickering oil-lamp.

'Jose has had Alphonso killed. He'll know that you're here. You killed two of his men up on the mountain. So he'll be eager to kill you as well.'

'Thanks for the advice. But I can look after myself.'

'I don't want another death on my hands,' she said, bitterly.

'What do you mean – another death?' asked Rand, puzzled.

They were the only two left in the dining-room. Alicia pushed her hair aside impatiently, revealing the disfigured side of her face.

'My sister was killed by Jose,' she said, tonelessly.

'Your sister?'

'She was left in the camp while I made my escape. To get even with me, Jose killed her.'

'Oh, no.'

'That's not the full story. He sent me her ear to show that he had indeed killed her. There was a blemish on the ear which she had received when we were children and she cut herself on a scythe. So his messenger was telling the truth.'

'The bastard.'

'So I want to make sure that you are safely

out of the way before I put my plan into action.'

'What plan?'

'Jose has always wanted me for himself. When I told him that I wasn't interested he threw some hot fat in my face. That's how I got this.' She touched the disfigured side of her face. 'The message I received was that he is still interested in me. So I'm going back to the camp. I'll go to bed with him. Then when he's asleep I'll kill him.'

CHAPTER 17

The following morning Rand rose early. There was no one moving in the hotel when he let himself out through a side door. He was about to visit someone who might just conceivably stop Alicia from committing suicide.

He arrived at the church before there was

any sign of anyone moving around although he knew that early-morning mass would be beginning soon. In fact the priest had seen him arrive and opened the door of the church as he went up the steps towards it.

'I wish the gates of heaven were as easy to open as this door,' said the priest. 'You're welcome to come inside. Unless there's something you wish to see me about, my son?'

'Actually, there is, Father. I want to try to stop somebody from committing murder. The deed will inevitably lead to her own death.'

The priest's welcoming smile changed to a look of concern as he led Rand through the church into a small chapel.

'I think you'd better tell me the whole story,' was the priest's advice.

Rand started telling him about Jose and how he had killed Alicia's sister.

'Yes, I heard about it,' said the priest. 'Jose will surely burn in hell.'

'Well, Alicia intends to see that he gets

113

there quicker than he normally would have done. She is going up to his camp to kill him.'

'Oh, no,' said the shocked priest. 'So that's why she hasn't come to confession for a while,' he added, half to himself. 'She's always been a regular churchgoer since she escaped from Jose's camp.'

'Well, I aim to stop her from going back to Jose's camp,' said Rand.

'I applaud your intention,' said the priest. 'But Alicia is a very determined young lady. When she makes up her mind to do something, she will not easily be diverted from her decision. Even though it means breaking the law.'

'There might be a way out of the dilemma,' said Rand.

'I hope there is,' said the priest, fervently.

Later in the morning Rand was again at his desk, finishing his task of drawing the posters for Perez. From time to time he kept glancing at his pocket-watch. Perez came in to bring him a cup of coffee.

'She hasn't come yet,' the lieutenant said.

'No. She promised she would come to see me before going up to Jose's camp.'

'She's a determined young lady. Perhaps she's decided to go ahead with her plan.'

Why did people keep on telling him that she was a determined person? He knew from first-hand experience that it was true. Look at the way she had seized her opportunity to escape from Jose's camp once she'd made up her mind to do so.

'Her brother, Christian, is a sergeant in the army,' said Perez. 'He's a keen soldier.'

'Alicia did mention her brother, Chris,' said Rand absently, as he listened for any sound of her approaching footsteps along the corridor.

They eventually arrived later in the morning. She knocked at the door and came in. Rand noted that she was wearing clothes which would be suitable for climbing the mountain. She was wearing a woollen dress, leather boots and a multicoloured cloak.

'I've come to say goodbye.' She stood in front of him, holding out her hand, formally.

Rand stood up.

'The last time we said good-bye you kissed me. Don't I get the same treatment now?'

For a moment uncertainty registered on her face.

'You think we should kiss?'

'I certainly do.'

It was a lingering kiss that reminded Rand of the kiss when they had parted at the end of their adventure on the mountainside.

When she broke away, she stood facing him. Her breasts heaved as she regained her composure. Eventually she said:

'I suppose you think that just by kissing me you will make me change my mind about killing Jose?'

'No.'

'That's good, because you won't make me change my mind.'

'Oh, yes, I will.'

Her whole attitude spelled defiance.

'And how do you propose to do that?'

'Because I'm telling you not to go and kill Jose.'

'You're what?' Her demeanour changed from the hostile manner which she had adopted since coming into the room. Her face suddenly lit up into a smile.

She was standing with the scarred side of her face towards the door and the good side was caught by the light from the window. Not for the first time Rand was struck by her beauty.

'I'm telling you, because I'm your husband,' he stated.

'You're – what?'

'We went through a ceremony in Jose's camp, remember. We're man and wife.'

'Don't be ridiculous. That marriage was a farce. It's not legal.'

'Oh, yes, it is. I went to see Father Gomez in his church this morning. I explained to him about the ceremony. He said that Mendez is a bona fide priest. That he is entitled to marry people. Therefore you see, you and I are married.'

'It's not true.' For the first time there was uncertainty in her attitude.

'So, since we're man and wife, I have no intention of allowing my wife to go on a journey which will inevitably result in her death,' Rand continued remorselessly.

'But the marriage was made under duress,' she protested.

'I asked Father Gomez about that. He said a large percentage of marriages in Mexico were arranged marriages. Many of them were made under duress. It doesn't make any difference to their legal position.'

She sat down on the spare chair in the office. For the first time Rand realized that he might be winning. However, her next words dashed his hopes.

'This is just a game to you, isn't it? You're saying this because you want to stop me getting killed. I understand that. But it's still a game. You've no intention of holding me to our marriage vows.'

'Of course I want to stop you from killing yourself,' snapped Rand. There was more anger in his voice than he had intended.

'All right, two can play games.' She stood up.

'What do you mean?'

'You say we're man and wife? I'll come to your hotel with you now and we can really be man and wife. That way I wouldn't dare to go to Jose's camp and get myself killed because I could be committing the mortal sin of killing an unborn child.'

Rand stared at her. Things weren't working out as he had planned. He had assumed she would fall in with his suggestion that since she was his wife she would obey his command. In Mexico the husband's word was law – much more so than in America. But now she had turned the tables on him. She stood in front of him, having reverted to her original attitude of defiance. This time, though, there was a gleam of success in her eye.

'Well?' She had put her hands on her hips in an age-old attitude, this time to emphasize her victory over him.

Could he let her go to certain death? He had no doubt that if she walked out of the room alone she would put her plan into action. They seemed to stand facing each other for ages, although it was probably only a couple of minutes. Eventually she turned away from him. As far as she was concerned the contest was over. She reached for the door-handle and was about to open it when Rand's words stopped her.

'We'll go back to the hotel together.'

CHAPTER 18

Late on the following morning twelve soldiers rode out of Limos. All wore the uniform of the Mexican army except Rand, who was dressed in civilian clothes. He and Christian were at the head of the column.

Perez had unhesitatingly agreed with Rand's suggestion that he should take a small party of soldiers to the poppy-fields. One of the reasons for Perez's instant acceptance of Rand's offer was that he saw it as a possible step for promotion for him to become mayor. If Rand and soldiers succeeded in destroying the poppy-fields he would be the one who would claim the glory, since it had been his decision to send them there.

Rand had pointed out that destroying the source of Jose's revenue would force him to change his style of living. He would no longer be able to live in the camp up on the mountain. When Rand had been led to the camp he had been surprised to see how well-fed the community was. When he had thought about it he didn't see how, by robbing a few hill-farmers of their sheep, the outlaws and their families could look so well fed. In fact the children looked better dressed and fed than some he had noticed in Limos. Later, when he had learned that Jose was responsible for controlling the supply of opium from the poppy-fields, the reason for the camp's affluence became apparent.

Rand had impressed on Perez before they set off that while he and his raiding party were away, the lieutenant should prepare the rest of his soldiers for a battle with Jose's men.

'With the source of Jose's supply of money cut off, he'll be forced to abandon his camp. He'll come down from the mountain. That's when you'll have your chance to finish off the outlaws once and for all.'

'You attend to the poppy-fields, I'll see to the outlaws,' said Perez, with a wide smile. He then asked Rand whether he needed anything extra to the normal army equipment he had requested.

'I'll want a couple of spare horses, in case there are any mishaps. I'll also want some dynamite and detonators.'

'I can get those from the stores. That won't be a problem.'

'The men will have to take provisions for at least a few days. Two water-bottles each and some rations.'

'I'll see that's done.'

'How far do you reckon it is to the poppy-fields?'

'About thirty miles. Of course you'll be riding along the plain, so you should make good time.'

'Thirty miles? So we should be there by this time tomorrow.'

Perez smiled. 'This is the Mexican army. Your American cavalry might be able to ride thirty miles and then fight a battle at the end of it, but unfortunately our soldiers are not such well-trained horsemen.'

'Well, we'll see how it goes,' said Rand enigmatically.

When they eventually rode out of the camp, Rand was surprised at how many people had gathered to see them off. He had hoped that their mission would have been kept comparatively secret. Instead, there seemed almost as many people gathered as there had been when Alphonso had been killed. So there went any chance of Jose not finding out about the purpose of his mission. Jose's spies would carry the news back up to his camp that a small party of soldiers, headed by the American officer, had left the town and headed south. Jose would immediately guess that they were heading for the poppy-fields. His instant reaction would be to gather together a war party of his own. Their destination, too, would be the poppy-fields. The one advantage that Rand and the soldiers would have over the outlaws would be that they would have several hours' start. Not only that, but they would be riding on the plain, where they should make good time. Whereas Jose and his outlaws would be travelling along the mountain paths, which would definitely slow their progress.

There was one more surprise in store for Rand before they rode out of the town. Many of the womenfolk had gathered on the low hill where Rand had stood when Alphonso had been shot. As the soldiers came opposite the spot, some of the women began to run towards them. The soldiers reined in their horses. Rand was forced to follow suit.

He realized the purpose of their halt when the women pinned ribbons on their husband or boyfriend. The ceremony of the pinning of the ribbon was followed by a kiss. The girlfriends and wives were saying farewell to their menfolk in what was obviously a Mexican tradition. Rand instinctively found himself looking round for Alicia. To his disappointment there was no sign of her.

The last soldier had been given his ribbon and they were about to ride off. Rand glanced round for the last time to see whether there was any sign of Alicia. She was nowhere in sight. The soldiers looked at him expectantly. He raised his right arm to give the sign that they should ride, when suddenly there was a shout from behind him. He turned in the saddle.

Alicia was racing towards them. She was holding a ribbon in her hand. Rand knew that he had a broad smile on his face as he jumped down from his horse to greet her. But what the hell!

'It took me ages to find a ribbon,' she gasped, as she stood in front of him and pinned it to his shirt.

Rand was aware that all eyes were on them as he took her in his arms and kissed her.

'That's so that you'll remember me,' she said, when they eventually broke apart.

CHAPTER 19

Rand and his soldiers made good time riding along the plain. During the first day they only had one brief stop. When Rand finally called a halt about an hour before sunset he guessed they had probably covered about twenty miles. Which wasn't bad for any group of horsemen. Indeed, he was pleasantly surprised at the professionalism of the patrol. They kept closely together, there were no requests for extra halts for water, and they even refrained from talking – which was an achievement for the normally garrulous Mexicans.

After they had devoured their supper of tortillas and beans Rand called them together. They sat round him and listened to what he had to say.

'Some time tomorrow afternoon we should arrive at the poppy-fields. When we see them we won't go galloping in to attack the outlaws who are controlling it. If we did their guards would easily pick us off. So we stay out of sight of the guards. The plan is that I ride in alone to find out what I can about how the place is guarded. I hope that I shall be able to ride back, so that we can then use our knowledge of how the place is guarded to ride in and destroy it.'

The following morning they set off early. After they had ridden for half a dozen or so miles Rand called a halt. While the men were having a short break he was scanning the horizon with his telescope. After a few moments he gave a grunt of satisfaction.

'Can you see anything?' Christian asked.

Rand's answer was to give him the telescope. Christian focused on a low ridge, several miles ahead.

'I can't see anything,' he announced.

'There's a sentry to the left. There's probably another one nearby. Where there's one sentry you'll always find another.'

'So probably the poppy-fields are the other side of the ridge,' said Christian, thoughtfully.

'That's what I would expect,' answered Rand. 'Although I've seen the sentry, I don't think he'll have seen us. Not unless he has a powerful telescope like this.'

'What do we do next?' demanded Christian.

'You and your men will hide in that stand of trees.' He pointed to a small wood about half a mile to their left. 'You will stay there until I come back. I shall hope to be back some time tomorrow if everything goes according to plan. Oh, and make sure the men clean their guns. A few of them look as though they haven't been cleaned for some time.'

'It will give the men something to do while you are away,' remarked Christian.

Having ensured that the men were safely hidden from any strangers who might be using the path on the plain, Rand set out for the ridge where the sentry was stationed. Although he was reasonably sure that the sentry would not shoot at him before giving the customary warning, nevertheless he experienced a few moments of unease before he eventually heard the command:

'Stay where you are, *señor.*'

Rand did so.

Another order followed.

'Now throw your rifle on the floor.'

Again Rand obeyed.

Satisfied, the sentry issued another order.

'Now ride up towards me slowly. Keeping both hands on the reins.'

When Rand reached the top of the ridge

he realized that his assumption about there being two sentries had been correct. Both had their rifles trained on him. Both gave the unmistakable impression of men who were used to handling guns and who would use them if necessary.

'Now, perhaps you will explain what you are doing in this remote part of the world, *señor*,' said the first sentry, who was obviously the spokesman.

'My name is Lieutenant Rand of the United States army. I've come to see your leader on official business.'

There was a silence. The sort of silence in which a lieutenant can become extremely uncomfortable under the hostile gaze of two sentries, particularly when their guns are trained on him.

'Have you any proof that you are in the United States army?'

Rand slowly took his identification disk from around his neck. He handed it to the nearest sentry. The Mexican examined it carefully before handing it back to him.

'What's to have prevented you from shooting this person named Lieutenant Rand, and stealing his identity?'

It was a good question. In fact it was such a good question that for a moment Rand didn't supply an answer. When he did so his attitude had changed. He was no longer the insubordinate and the sentries his superiors. He turned the tables with his blistering verbal attack.

'Listen, you. If you don't take me to the person in charge immediately, I will see that you will be relieved of your duties as sentries as from this moment. You will spend not days, but months, cleaning the latrines. Instead of this nice, easy post you will be made to work until every bone in your bodies aches. Your position will be the lowest of the low. People will spit on you as they pass. Every day you will regret not taking me to your leader immediately when I ordered you to do so.'

He had once heard a sergeant giving a similar speech in the army camp. It had worked then. It worked now as the sentries' attitude instantly changed.

'A thousand pardons, *señor.* I will take you to Scarpia.'

CHAPTER 20

The camp was clearly visible once the sentry had led Rand over the ridge. It was situated in a flat, open space. Rand immediately realized that its situation, with low hills on either side, would make it extremely difficult for an enemy attack to succeed.

The camp was a conventional one with dozens of tents spaced out on the flat ground. The unusual buildings, however, which immediately held Rand's interest were the long wooden sheds which formed one side of the camp. Rand counted half a dozen sheds in all as he was led to the centre of the compound.

Rand's entry and the sentry's had caused considerable interest. Most of the people who had been walking around in the camp suddenly stopped and stared at them. Rand had the ridiculous notion that he should salute them as they passed.

One thing of interest which he filed away in his mind for future use was the fact that many of those who stopped and stared were Indians. He guessed they were Apaches. So that was where Scarpia got his cheap labour from, which he would need to run a camp of this size.

Scarpia himself was seated in the largest tent. Rand was led inside by the sentry. To Rand's surprise Scarpia, who was alone, was playing solitaire. Scarpia waved his hand to dismiss the sentry.

'Sit down, Mr – er...'

'Rand. Lieutenant Rand.'

He sat opposite Scarpia. For some vague reason he had expected the Mexican to be a comparatively young man, but Scarpia, with his white beard, would probably be in his sixties. He held a card in his hand before eventually putting it down on another card. He sighed.

'You know, Lieutenant, I hardly ever succeed with this game of solitaire. Do you play cards?'

'Now and then.'

Scarpia studied him for the first time since he had entered the tent.

'Now and then,' he said, thoughtfully. 'Do you play poker?'

'Yes.'

'Maybe we'll have a game before you leave. That's the one thing I miss, having lived away from civilization for some time – a game of poker.'

So Scarpia had set up his illegal trade some time ago. It fitted with the information Rand had received from the soldiers who had brought drugs into the army camp. That there had been a regular supply-line for several years.

'But you haven't come here to play cards. Maybe you could explain why you are here.'

Rand went into his carefully prepared speech.

'Your supply of opium to our army camp in United States seems to have decreased recently. As you probably know we have many soldiers who are dependent on the drug. I'm here to find out whether there has indeed been a decrease in the supply.'

'I'm rather surprised at this announcement. In fact I'm very surprised at it.'

'Maybe it's just a temporary hitch. That's what I'd like to find out.'

'I see.' Scarpia stroked his beard thoughtfully. 'Have you been in touch with Jose? He's our middleman.'

'I believe his camp is up in the mountains. I thought it would be better to come here.'

'Yes, well, maybe you've done the right thing. You've come from Limos?'

'Yes.'

'In that case you'll probably be hungry. I'll arrange a meal for you. Then I'll take you on a tour of the poppy-fields themselves. You'll be able to confirm that at least

at this end the supply of opium is as constant as ever.'

Rand was taken to a large tent where there
were several long tables. The tent reminded
him of the army dining-room. One major
difference, however, was that when he had a
meal in the camp there would also be a few
dozen soldiers at the tables. Here, however,
he was the only one.

He was served a steak by a teenage
Mexican girl.

'I hope it's been cooked as you like it,' she
said. 'My mother cooked it and she said all
Americans like their steak with the blood
still in sight.'

Rand smiled.

'It looks perfect to me.' So it proved. In
fact he had a pang of guilt when he reflected
that he was enjoying a perfect meal while
Christian and his soldiers would be on army
rations.

After the meal, and when Rand had
assured the Mexican girl, whose name, he
discovered, was Rosita, that the meal was

indeed perfect, he was shown back to Scarpia's tent.

'Now I will demonstrate that everything at this end of the supply line is exactly as it has always been. First you will visit the poppy-fields. Unfortunately I cannot take you there myself because old age prevents me from riding a horse. But my manager will take you there.'

Rand was introduced to the manager, Arturo. Normally Rand wasn't quick to judge a man on first impressions. He had discovered over the years that they could be misleading. But there was something about Arturo to which he took an instant dislike. Maybe it was his overly fawning attitude to Scarpia. Or maybe it was his sly glances in Rand's direction which seemed to suggest that Arturo wasn't entirely convinced that Rand was a genuine seeker after knowledge about how the opium was supplied.

'It's about twenty minutes ride to the poppy-fields,' Arturo informed Rand.

They rode in silence. Rand noted that they

were riding south, away from the wood where Christian and his soldiers were hiding. When they crossed over a ridge Rand could see the poppy-fields. He was amazed at how extensive they were. A white carpet of poppies stretched into the distance.

As they rode nearer Rand could distinguish the people who were gathering the poppies. There were dozens of them bending down picking the flowers. Arturo called a halt when they were on the edge of the first field so that Rand could savour the activity. All the poppy-gatherers were women. They wore identical white smocks with a large pocket sewn into the front. Into this pocket they would drop the poppy they had just picked. They moved from plant to plant without straightening up. Rand noted that most of them were Indians – presumably Apaches.

This fact was confirmed by Arturo.

'The Apaches will pick the poppies all day for a few pesos. When we started off we employed Mexican women but they soon refused to pick the poppies for the money we were giving them.'

Rand noticed another fact, that at the end of each row of women there was a guard standing. They held whips in their hands. As he watched, one of the women half-stumbled. The guard was on her like a flash, his whip striking her across her back. Her scream of pain could be heard from the spot where Rand was standing.

A smile of satisfaction spread over Arturo's face.

'You've got to keep them under control or they will take advantage of you,' he observed.

Rand knew that given the chance he would take great pleasure in smashing that smug expression with his fist.

'Have you seen everything you want to see?' demanded Arturo, insolently.

'Yes,' replied Rand.

They rode back to the camp. Rand knew he was no nearer to forming a plan to destroy Scarpia's empire. In fact the task looked a pretty hopeless one. In the first place he would have to destroy all the poppies which, now that he had seen the extent of the fields, would be an impossible task. The only alternative would be to destroy the buildings where the poppies were actually converted into opium.

Arturo led Rand back into Scarpia's tent.

'I've shown him the fields,' he announced.

'What did you think of them?' demanded Scarpia.

'They were very impressive,' Rand answered, truthfully.

'Yes, they are, aren't they,' said Scarpia. He dismissed Arturo with a wave of his hand. 'Now I'll show you the production side of the operation.'

He led Rand out of the tent and towards the low buildings which Rand had observed when he had first entered the camp. Several Mexican women were washing clothes outside their tents. Some of the younger ones glanced appreciatively at the tall American as they passed.

Scarpia noted their glances and smiled.

'You wouldn't think that not too many years ago I too had admiring glances from young ladies.'

He led Rand into the first of the buildings. He clapped his hands and the half-dozen workers stopped what they were doing.

'I'm just going to show Lieutenant Rand what we do here,' he stated. He led Rand to a table in the centre of the room where a strange-looking contraption had pride of place.

'This is the crusher,' Scarpia explained. 'It is the most important piece of our equipment. We also have two more in the other buildings,' he added.

Rand examined the crusher. It consisted of a large metal drum with probably a couple of dozen small holes on the outside.

'The operator puts the poppy-plant inside these holes. When each hole has been filled he turns the handle,' explained Scarpia. He called to a sturdy Mexican who was stripped to the waist. 'Perhaps you will give us a demonstration, Stephano.'

The Mexican grasped the handle and began to turn it slowly. It was obviously hard work since the drum moved only about an inch at a time. As the drum rotated a colourless liquid came out of a narrow hole. The liquid moved slowly along a narrow tube into a cuplike container.

'It takes about a thousand poppies to make a thimbleful of opium,' Scarpia informed him. 'So that's why we need all those poppies in the fields. Also, because of the weather, we only get one harvest. So everything has to be gathered and prepared in a few short weeks. As you can see, we are in the middle of the process now.'

Rand stored the information away for future reference. If the production could somehow be halted in the next few days it would mean that it couldn't be restarted until the following year.

'The ladies you see around you are storing the liquid in bottles and labelling them. It is important that our suppliers have correctly labelled bottles. Of course some of these bottles will go to San Caldiz where the opium will be used by the apothecaries as morphine to help to treat various illnesses. As you know, Lieutenant, the use of the hypodermic in the last few years has greatly increased the use of the drug for medicinal purposes.'

'But there's considerably more money to be made in using the opium as an illegal drug?'

'I would say that there is about twenty times the amount of money to be made that way,' Scarpia informed Rand, as he led him out of the building.

CHAPTER 21

A couple of hours later Rand was on his way to play poker with Scarpia. The Mexican had told him that it would be too late for him to start back to Limos that day. He had advised him to start back early the following morning. In the meantime he had insisted that Rand should have another meal. This time he was again the only one in the tent which he had labelled the canteen. He was again served by Rosita.

This time she brought him rabbit-pie accompanied by hot tortillas.

'Your mother is an excellent cook, Rosita,' he informed her.

'If you stay here we will soon fatten you up,' she retorted.

'Sadly I'll have to stay thin, since I'll be going away shortly.'

'You should marry a Mexican woman, she will soon make you put on weight,' said Rosita, as she brought in some fruit and cream for dessert.

He almost retorted: I have. But to avoid any lengthy explanation he did not reply. After all, his marriage had probably been one of the strangest on record. He had married Alicia to prevent himself being killed by Jose. Then, when he could have announced that the whole marriage was a sham, he had insisted that it was real in order to save Alicia from being killed by Jose.

After all that, he admitted to himself he didn't feel like a married man. If he decided to return to America he had no doubt that a magistrate would annul the marriage on the grounds of its being made under duress. Of course it would mean leaving Alicia behind. There was no doubt that it would be a big wrench. Although he had only known her for a few days and they had had one night of unbridled passion he realized she was a loyal person who would stick to him through thick and thin if he decided to let the marriage stand without contesting it.

He had agreed to play cards with Scarpia in the hope that he might yet be able to find a solution for his other problem: how to destroy the opium factory. A vague idea had formed in his mind that he could blow up the sheds using dynamite. This would certainly put a stop to Scarpia's opium production since the important implements, and crushers, would be put out of action. He realized, however, that such an assault would be fraught with danger.

In the first place it would have to be carried out at night, because any daylight battle between Christian's men and Scarpia's guards would invariably lead to the former being defeated, since the guards were stationed at vantage points around the camp. In addition there was the problem of actually destroying the poppy-fields. Assuming he was successful in blowing up the sheds with dynamite, Scarpia would soon be able to go back into production using the poppies which had still to be harvested. Of course the production would be on a much smaller scale and the poppies would have to be crushed by hand. But it would not be an insurmountable problem. There were hand-crushers available which were used to crush garlic-cloves. These could be used to crush the poppy-seed.

The more he thought about the task which

he had undertaken, the more he realized its hopelessness.

At about the same time that Rand was thinking about Alicia, she was also thinking about him. He had been gone barely twenty-four hours and yet she was already missing him terribly. She had been stunned when he had insisted that the marriage ceremony up in the mountains had been a genuine one. She had been amazed when he had suggested that since they were a married couple they should spend the night together.

Of course Rand's motives were glaringly obvious. He couldn't bear the thought of her sacrificing herself to Jose: a sacrifice which would inevitably lead to her death.

It meant, of course, that he cared about her. In fact he cared a lot about her since he had taken the trouble of consulting Father Gomez in order to confirm that their marriage was legal. Did he love her? Well, maybe he did. There had been moments in their night of passion when tenderness had taken over. And in those moments he had held her in his arms. One such moment had been in the early morning when it had been light enough for her to see him. And the expression she had caught on his face was one of absolutely contentment. She was prepared to swear on the Bible that she was not mistaken.

But now there was something niggling in the back of her mind about Rand. As she went about her daily tasks she tried to pinpoint it, but it eluded her. She eventually decided that maybe she was following the wrong track. She had been thinking of events which had happened in the past, whereas she should be concentrating on something which was going to happen in the future. She had more than a little gypsy blood in her and it was that side of her nature which had helped her, on rare occasions, to foresee events before they were going to happen. Now she suddenly had a premonition that something terrible was going to happen to Rand. The vision was so real that she almost shouted out a warning to him, even though he was miles away.

Her sister-in-law, Maria, was startled by the suddenness with which Alicia burst into the kitchen. She was even more surprised when Alicia announced that she would be taking her horse and riding out to join Rand.

'But he's gone with the soldiers to the poppy-fields,' protested Maria.

'I know. But I think he's in great danger.' Alicia was changing into her riding-boots as she spoke.

Maria could read the determination on Alicia's face.

'All right,' she conceded, 'I'll get you some food to take with you. And I'll fill your water-bottles. And good luck,' she added.

'I'll need it,' Alicia retorted.

CHAPTER 22

In fact Rand could have done with a fair share of luck as his lack of winnings against Scarpia signified. When he had eventually entered Scarpia's tent he had found the Mexican seated at the table playing solitaire.

Scarpia looked up.

'Did you have an enjoyable meal?' he enquired, politely.

'It was excellent,' said Rand, as he took his seat opposite the Mexican.

'Rosita's mother is an excellent cook. I think I can blame my expanded waistline on her.'

Rand smiled dutifully.

'Not only have you had excellent food but you will be able to take some other memento back to Limos to remind you of our hospitality,' said Scarpia, blandly.

Was Rand mistaken, or was there some hidden threat behind the words. It had seemed an innocent enough observation, but Rand thought he detected a hint of a threat.

'You mentioned that we were going to play poker.'

'That's right. And in deference to the fact that officers in the army are notoriously poorly paid, I will supply you with the funds with which to play.' Rand was about to protest, but Scarpia waved any protestation aside. 'Anyhow, I aim to win the money back, so maybe you won't be fortunate enough to take a great deal back with you.'

Scarpia produced a pouch from a drawer. He tipped a pile of American silver dollar coins on to the table. He began to divide them into two equal piles.

Rand stared at the growing piles. If he won any of this money he certainly wouldn't want to keep it. To him it represented tainted money. It stood for the misery which he had witnessed at first hand of good men whose lives had been ruined by the drug which was being processed a short distance from where they were sitting.

Scarpia finished counting out the money.

'There, one hundred dollars each.' He pushed one pile across the table towards Rand. 'We'll play draw-poker. You can change any or all of your cards. There is no maximum stake. Any questions?'

'No, none.'

They started to play. At first Rand had regarded the game as just a means of passing time. He had conceded to Scarpia's whim in the hope that by prolonging his stay he might be able to come up with an answer to his problem – how to destroy Scarpia's evil empire. He realized there was an element of risk involved in it, since presumably Jose would be on his way to report to Scarpia that the American was not what he seemed. That in fact he was a spy.

Rand had calculated that since Jose would have started several hours after him, and also that he would be following the mountain trails, then the earliest that Jose could arrive would be some time the next morning. Which meant that if he started at daybreak, as Scarpia had agreed, he should be able to rejoin Christian's men in time.

The first few hands were of little interest. It was soon obvious to Rand that Scarpia was waiting for one big hand, and that he would put a sizeable bet on it. The time dragged on. Although the hands so far had mostly consisted of pairs or at the most a run or a flush, Scarpia's pile of money had definitely increased, while his had shrunk. At first Rand told himself that it didn't matter if Scarpia won; after all it was his money. But as the game progressed Rand found that he became more anxious to avoid losing. At the end of the game he wanted to present Scarpia with at least the money with which he had started.

Rand guessed that they had been playing for over an hour when the first sign of a promising hand came his way. He had been dealt three sevens, a four and a ten. If he could be successful and draw another seven, or a ten, he would have the best hand he had seen so far. In fact he drew a ten. He had a full house. This hand should be able to take some of Scarpia's money from him.

Rand studied Scarpia's face. As usual his opponent had given little away. He had drawn three cards. This might mean that he had a pair which he would be hoping to improve upon.

The betting started as usual with one dollar. The pot grew until there was over twenty dollars in it. Scarpia kept glancing at Rand, but he wasn't going to give anything away; he had played poker with some of the best players in the regiment, and so had learned the value of keeping an expression-less face.

When the pot had increased to around thirty dollars, Scarpia called. Rand showed him his hand. Scarpia's sigh of disappoint-ment told him that he had won. Scarpia's hand in fact consisted of two pairs.

Rand moved the coins across the table. It

was evident that he was now winning. At that moment an attractive Mexican girl came in carrying two glasses of tequila. She handed one to Scarpia and the other to Rand.

'Thank you, Carmen,' said Scarpia. 'She's one of my granddaughters,' he explained, with a hint of pride in his voice. He began to drink his tequila.

'She's a very pretty girl,' said Rand, also sipping his drink.

'A compliment from an American will keep her in good spirits for the rest of the day,' said Scarpia. He finished his drink and handed the empty glass back to Carmen.

Rand, too, finished his drink. He was pleased that at last he had shown an increase in the stake that Scarpia had given him. They played a few hands but none of them was worth Rand betting on. As they played Scarpia looked at him with what seemed a new interest. Was he trying to read his mind to discover whether he had a winning hand? Up until now Scarpia had glanced at him casually from time to time, concentrating for the most part on his own hand. But now he definitely seemed to be studying Rand more. Maybe he was annoyed that he had won the only biddable hand to date.

Scarpia dealt him a pair of twos. When Rand drew three cards he couldn't improve on it. Normally he would have bet a few dollars on it in the hope that Scarpia didn't even have a pair. For some odd reason he pushed forward ten dollars towards the centre of the table. What was he doing? Scarpia had already put two dollars in the pot, showing that he intended bidding on his hand. Why was he throwing ten dollars away like this? Of course it wasn't his own money, so it didn't really matter. But a few minutes ago he was concentrating on the game as if his life depended on winning it. Now his attitude had suddenly changed.

Scarpia's response to his bet was a smile. Rand put ten dollars into the pot to see his hand. Scarpia held a pair of aces. His expression perfectly mirrored someone gloating as he gathered his winnings.

Rand muttered to himself that he must pull his socks up.

'Did you say something?' Scarpia enquired.

'No, it's nothing. I've just got a bit of a thick head. It must be the tequila.' *It must be the tequila.* The thought hit him like a thunderbolt. The tequila had been drugged.

He had to get out of here. He rose to his feet, holding on to the table for support. Scarpia, who until then had only had one head now seemed to have grown half a dozen more. They were all grinning at him. Rand started to move towards the door. He felt that his whole life depended on getting out of the tent. He managed a few unsteady steps, then a strange thing happened. The door was suddenly no longer where he thought it had been. Somebody must have moved it. In fact somebody must be moving the whole tent because it was spinning round him like a top. It was all too difficult to keep your balance in such circumstances. He did the only thing that a reasonable person would do – he collapsed on to the floor.

He was aware of a couple of people carrying him back to his chair. Where had they come from? They weren't here when he had been playing cards. He was also vaguely aware of Scarpia talking.

'Listen, gringo, if you can hear me. As you now realize, you have been drugged. It's no more than you deserve. You came here thinking I would swallow your cock-and-bull story about checking up on the American side of our distribution. I can tell you explicitly that there's nothing wrong with it. No, you are a spy, sent by your friends to try to find out as much as you can about how we produce the opium. Well, you've seen it. Not that it will benefit you, since you are shortly going to die. Normally one of my guards would be happy to carry out the execution, but I will wait a short while and hand that privilege over to Jose. He will be arriving here shortly to tell me whether he has been successful in the assassination of Alphonso.

'Don't you realize that Jose comes here once every few months. The last time he came here all he talked about was you, and what he would do to you when he finally caught up with you. You should be honoured, gringo, that we spent so much of our time talking about you.'

Rand's head slumped forward. It was obvious that he was unconscious. If it hadn't been that two men were holding him he would have slid off his chair.

'Take him to the prison,' said Scarpia, contemptuously.

CHAPTER 23

Christian's soldiers, who had already spent one night in the wood, were getting restless.

'Can't we go into the camp and fight it out with the guys who are supplying the opium,' suggested one of the privates.

There was a murmur of agreement.

'Rand told us to wait until he comes back,' countered Christian.

'What if something has happened?' said another. 'He's been gone over twenty-four hours. Maybe whoever's in charge of running the opium business has taken Rand prisoner. He might even be dead by now.'

'I hope not, for Alicia's sake,' said Christian fervently.

Their conversation was suddenly brought to an abrupt end by an apparition. It was an Indian who seemed to have materialized out of the ground. The soldiers instinctively reached for the guns.

'It's all right,' said the Indian, an Apache named Lightning Strikes Twice, 'I'm a friend.'

'How did you know we were here?' demanded Christian.

'We've been watching you from the time you came here.'

'Who's we?' asked a surprised Christian.

'A few dozen of my friends.'

'Where are they now?' enquired one of the soldiers.

'They're in Scarpia's camp.'

'Who's Scarpia?' enquired Christian.

'He's the boss. The one who runs the opium trade.'

'You say your Apache friends all work for him?' asked a soldier.

'Oh, no. Our wives work for him. We men are mostly idle.'

'It sounds like an ideal life,' said one of the soldiers to general laughter.

'It's not true,' retorted the Apache, beginning to get angry. 'Our wives work in the fields all day gathering the poppies. They work so hard that when they come to our tents they are too tired for anything. We men have to cook the meals and see to the children.'

'I suppose the women are too tired for other things as well,' suggested one of the soldiers.

'What do you think?' snapped Lightning

Strikes Twice.

'So you've got a problem,' said Christian. 'How can we help you?'

'We are not the ones who've got a problem,' stated the Apache. 'You are the ones with the problem.'

'What do you mean?' demanded Christian.

'The tall American who came into the camp yesterday.'

'Yes, what about him?'

'He's been taken prisoner by Scarpia.'

'Oh, no,' groaned Christian.

'Oh, yes. And worse, there's no chance of him escaping because he's been drugged.'

'Lieutenant Rand has been drugged?'

'Yes, if that's his name.'

'How do you know this?'

'Scarpia's grand-daughter, Carmen, is friendly with my daughter, Lily of the Valley. She told Lily that Lieutenant Rand had been drugged.'

'If Rand is a prisoner then it's up to us to try to rescue him,' said one of the soldiers. There was a chorus of approval from the other soldiers.

'If you attack the camp now you will all be killed,' stated the Apache.

'What would you suggest?' asked Christian.

'He's an Indian,' said one of the soldiers. 'What would he know about fighting the Mexicans?'

'One of our leaders was very successful against the Americans,' said the Apache.

'Who's he talking about?' asked a soldier.

'Geronimo,' supplied another.

'So what would you suggest?' Christian repeated the question.

'If you are going to attack the camp you must do it when the Mexicans are having their siesta.'

'That sounds reasonable,' said Christian, thoughtfully. 'What about the guards? Where are they?'

The Indian, who was sitting cross-legged on the ground, drew a circle in the dust.

'This is the camp. Scarpia has four guards. One at each corner of the camp.' He drew four crosses.

'Where is Scarpia's tent?'

'Here in the middle of the camp. You can't miss it.' He drew another cross.

'Is there anything else I should know about the camp?'

'There are six long sheds here.' He drew a line. 'These are where the opium is made.'

'I see,' said Christian thoughtfully.

'Your lieutenant is being held prisoner in the end shed.' He pointed to it.

'How many more soldiers has Scarpia got?' enquired one of the men.

'About a dozen. But they're not fighting soldiers. They just go around the place wearing soldiers' uniforms. Most of the time they just take our women,' said the Apache bitterly.

'So if our raid is successful,' said Christian, 'what will you get out of it? Your wives won't be working. They won't have a job.'

'Scarpia only pays them a slave's wage anyhow,' said the Apache. 'And if your raid is successful we'll get our wives back.'

CHAPTER 24

Alicia had ridden as fast as she had dared. She didn't know exactly how far away the poppy-fields were. She realized that she couldn't push the horse too fast since she would want to conserve its strength.

The prairie was deserted except for the occasional solitary rider, most of whom seemed to be riding towards Limos. One or two of them glanced curiously at a young woman who was riding alone, but apart from a friendly greeting, none of the riders bothered her.

One thing that did cause her concern, however, was the fact that in a couple of hours it would be dark. It would mean she would have to spend the night alone, on the prairie. She knew that wild animals roamed around at night. Particularly coyotes. They usually hunted in packs on the prairie. The thought of a pack of them coming across her in the night sent shivers down her spine.

Another worry which kept cropping up from time to time was how was she going to find the poppy-fields? She knew that they roughly lay some distance ahead, but there would be no signpost saying: 'Poppy Fields'. She could hardly stop one of the travellers and say: 'Excuse me, could you tell me the way to the fields where they make opium?' It was a problem which she knew she would have to resolve some time in the morning, because the sun wasn't far above the horizon and she knew that once the sun had set darkness would soon be upon her.

Suddenly she came to a conclusion about not spending a night on the plain. She would climb one of the mountain paths. Her decision was implemented when she saw a convenient path to her left. She turned her horse towards it.

Alicia told herself that by climbing the path she would be achieving two things. In the first place there was the obvious advantage in getting off the plain, and therefore avoiding any bands of coyotes; also, by going higher she might be able to spot the poppy-fields in the morning. Yes, it could definitely be of an advantage to her in the morning.

She climbed as far as she could while daylight lasted. She was eventually forced to dismount and tie the horse to a convenient tree where he could happily graze. Her own supper consisted of a chunk of bread and some goat's cheese, followed by an apple. Even such basic fare was quite tasty. She wondered why food eaten out in the open air is usually tastier than when eaten indoors. It was her last thought before she slipped into a sound sleep.

When she awoke in the morning it took her a few moments to get her bearings. She felt quite pleased that she had survived the night, even though she was feeling rather cold. Well, what did she expect, since she was roughly a thousand feet up the mountainside?

Her next observation was a curious one. She thought she heard voices. Surely she was mistaken. No two people would be coming along the path in this deserted part of the world, as early as this in the morning? She was not mistaken – there the voices were again.

The sound galvanized her into action. The last thing she wanted was to meet strangers. She hastily rolled up her blanket, untied the horse and proceeded to lead it up the mountain away from the path. She dragged the horse upwards as quickly as she could. From time to time she kept glancing behind to see whether there was any sign of the people whose voices had disturbed the silence of the mountainside.

There was a tree up ahead. It was an old stunted tree which was typical of the trees which dotted the mountainside, nevertheless if she could reach it before the strangers arrived at the spot where she had been spending the night she would be comparatively safe.

She gasped for breath as she dragged the horse up the few remaining yards. She had made it! The tree's foliage hid her and the horse from whoever would soon be moving along the path. Not only was she hidden, but by pushing some of the leaves aside she had a perfect view of the path below.

She was amazed when a couple of moments later the first of the riders came into sight. It was Jose. He was followed in single file by about half a dozen of his outlaws. One of them was Fernando, who had been responsible for Alphonso's death.

An exciting thought occurred to Alicia. Jose and his outlaws were obviously on their way to the poppy-fields. They were going to fetch their supply of opium. Well, here was the answer to her problem. All she had to do was to follow them at a safe distance and they would lead her to the fields. What a surprise would be in store for them when they discovered that Rand and his men had arrived there before them.

CHAPTER 25

In the soldier's camp Christian and his men were busy cleaning their guns. There was an expectant air about the camp. After a couple of days of inactivity there was at last the promise of some action.

'What about the dynamite?' asked one of the soldiers.

'I'll take charge of that,' said Christian. 'If what that Indian said is true we've got to try to destroy the five sheds.'

'The Indian said there were six sheds,' a soldier pointed out.

'Yes, but Rand is being held in the end one. We can hardly blow that one up as well.'

'So we attack the camp and while we are doing that you blow up the five sheds?'

'That's right.'

'So you'll need different lengths of fuse,'

the soldier informed him.

Christian hadn't thought of that but his face gave nothing away.

'Do you know anything about fuses, Manuel?'

'My father worked on the railway from Topez to San Caldiz. He had a lot to do with dynamite.'

Christian produced the fuses.

'So how long do you think the fuses should be to allow us to blow up the five sheds?'

Manuel examined the fuse wire.

'We'll want one long one to start, then the next one should be, say, two metres shorter. The next one two metres shorter again, and so on.'

'Perhaps you can cut the lengths,' suggested Christian.

Manuel set about cutting the fuses to the required lengths.

Is there anything else I've forgotten? Christian put the question to himself. No, there didn't seem to be anything. Of course if Rand were here the American would be in charge and then if anything went wrong it would be Rand's responsibility. But if the Indian was right, Rand was not going to be of any use in the forthcoming battle.

It was about that time that Rand was showing signs of stirring from his drugged sleep. The guard, who was sitting by the door of the hut, looked up from the comic book he had been reading. He opened the door and called out to the guard who was standing outside.

'The patient wants another dose of medicine.'

The ambiguous request set several courses of action moving. The guard called to a passing Mexican woman.

'Bianca, tell Scarpia that the American is recovering.'

Bianca hurried to Scarpia's tent where she passed on the information. Scarpia told Bianca to fetch Carmen. In a few minutes Carmen appeared accompanied by Lily of the Valley.

'What is she doing here?' Scarpia scowled at the Indian girl.

'She's my friend,' replied Carmen, stubbornly.

'Well, you can pick another friend,' snapped Scarpia. 'In the meantime I want you to prepare another drink for the American.'

'Do you want it about the same strength as the last one?'

'If he's just waking up, yes, I'd want it the same strength.'

Carmen and her friend left Scarpia's tent and headed for one of the huts. Carmen explained to the guard that she was on an errand for her grandfather. He let the two girls into the hut. Inside the hut were rows and rows of small bottles of the colourless opium. This was a storeroom in which there was none of the activity of the hut to which Rand had been led earlier.

Carmen chose a bottle which had already been started from a shelf.

'Oh, damn, I've forgotten to bring the tequila,' she said, in exasperation. 'You stay here while I go and fetch it,' she added.

She left the hut. When she had gone Lily of the Valley searched desperately around the hut. She eventually found what she was searching for – a bottle of water. She grabbed it and carried it to the table where the bottle of opium stood. She took the bottle of opium and went over to a waste-bin in the corner. She poured about half the opium into the bin. Then she replaced with water the opium she had tipped out. She hurried back to the shelf. She had just replaced the bottle of water when Carmen returned with the tequila.

Scarpia was waiting in the hut where Rand was being held prisoner. Carmen knocked and the two girls entered. Carmen handed Scarpia the glass.

Rand, who was still only partly awake, tried to focus on the glass.

'Time to take your medicine, gringo,' said Scarpia. 'If you don't the guard will shoot you. It will deprive Jose of the pleasure of doing so, but I'm sure the sight of your dead body will be sufficient compensation.'

Rand stared at the glass. For a moment it looked as though he was going to refuse to drink it. Scarpia motioned to the guard who stepped forward. The two girls gasped in horror as the guard held his revolver to Rand's head.

'You wouldn't want to spoil these young ladies' day would you, gringo, by having your brains scattered all over the floor?'

Rand shook his head as though trying to clear it. The four people in the hut stood in silence as he stared at the glass. The silence was shattered when Scarpia nodded to the guard and the unmistakable 'click' of the revolver followed.

'No!' screamed Lily of the Valley.

The sound of her scream seemed to stir some reaction in Rand. He stared half-comprehendingly at the four. Then his gaze settled on the glass. He stretched out his hand. Scarpia handed it to him.

'Drink it all up and you will have another nice sleep,' said Scarpia.

Rand emptied the glass. Everyone in the hut heaved a sigh of relief for their own reasons; Scarpia because he would like to hand over his prisoner alive to Jose; the guard because he had never killed a man before and he didn't like the idea of being an executioner; Carmen, because she couldn't stand the sight of blood – anybody's blood; and Lily of the Valley because she believed that since she had watered down the opium there was a slight chance that Rand would somehow be able to recover and be rescued by the soldiers her father had told her were going to attack the camp that afternoon.

CHAPTER 26

Alicia was happily following the outlaws. The only thing that marred her peace of mind was the nagging thought that some-thing tragic was going to happen to her beloved Rand. She tried to dismiss the thought. Maybe she had been overreacting when she had received the first intimation that something was wrong. Surely not. One of the times when she had been convinced that tragedy would strike was when her sister-in-law Maria had her first baby. She was utterly convinced that something dreadful would happen to the baby. Of course she had never told Maria. But when the baby was born her fears were justified. It was a terrible tragedy. The baby was born dead.

Of course Maria had had two children since then who were fit and healthy. The thought came unbidden – would she have children? There was no doubt that she would love to have at least two. She could imagine Rand as a father – he would be the ideal father, kind but firm. There was one snag though. What about the side of her face which had been burned by Jose? She wouldn't want her children to see that. Of course there was a good chance that it could be cured. There was old Mother Slone who lived in Limos. She was as old as Methuselah and as wise as Solomon, so they said. She treated all sorts of illnesses from broken bones – for which she used a paste called knit-bone – to skin complaints. Indeed, when she had met her in the market a few weeks ago she had told her that she could cure her facial disfigurement. At the time she had told the old woman that she wasn't interested. But since then things had changed. She had a husband and she would want to look her best for him. And who knew, she might even have the seed of a child in her womb.

She was day-dreaming so much that she hadn't noticed that the outlaws had disappeared from her sight. They had ridden round a bend about a hundred yards ahead. She instinctively spurred her horse to try to catch them up. The last thing she wanted was to lose them and as a result have to try to find the poppy-fields herself.

She realized her mistake the moment she

rode round the corner. The outlaws were waiting for her. Some of them had guns in their hands.

'So it's the lovely Alicia,' said Jose, with a nauseating smile. 'And delivered right into my hands.'

In the Indian camp, which was slightly apart from the Mexican tents, a heated argument was taking place.

'It'll be the best thing that will have happened to us,' stated Lightning Strikes Twice.

He was facing two of the elders and one young Apache named Wolf in the Mountains.

'But everything is perfect here,' protested one of the elders. 'The women are doing the work, and we have enough money to smoke our pipes in the evening.'

'It's all right for you,' said Wolf in the Mountains, angrily. 'We young braves don't smoke the pipe. We've got nothing to do all day.'

'Except to look after the children,'

Lightning Strikes Twice added sharply. 'This place has turned us into women.'

'If you help to destroy the poppy-fields, what are you going to do then?' asked the other elder.

'The Mexicans are going to build a rail-road from San Caldiz to Limos,' Lightning Strikes Twice informed them. 'They will want young men like us to build it. We will camp near Limos. We will be able to eat proper food again, not the rubbish that Scarpia allows us to eat.'

'It would be nice to eat proper food again,' agreed one of the elders.

'Then is it agreed?' demanded Lightning Strikes Twice.

'Let's smoke a pipe before we come to an agreement,' said one of the elders.

'We haven't time,' said Lightning Strikes Twice, irritably. 'The soldiers will be starting to move any time now. We've got to decide here and now: are we going to help to destroy Scarpia's opium trade.'

The two elders reluctantly raised their

hands. Wolf in the Mountains raised his hand far more eagerly.

Lightning Strikes Twice was quite correct: the soldiers were on the move. Christian knew exactly where the two guards on the ridge were stationed, and they were his first target. Fortunately there was ample cover as the soldiers crawled up the hillside. Christian headed for the first guard. His back was towards Christian which meant that he should be able to get quite close to him before the guard turned.

In fact Christian managed to get within touching distance before the soldier realized from a slight sound behind him that something was amiss. He swung round. The cry of warning he was about to deliver choked in his throat as Christian stabbed him in the heart.

Another soldier had similarly disposed of the other guard. Christian gathered his soldiers together. They were situated on top of the ridge with a clear view of the camp below. The scene seemed to be peaceful enough with some Mexican women going about their tasks. Then suddenly Christian gave a gasp of horror. He could see a different group of people. He recognized their leader as Jose. However it was not Jose who caused Christian's gasp of horror, but the person who was being led as a prisoner. It was his sister, Alicia.

What was she doing here? Had Jose brought her here from Limos? It didn't make sense; Jose would never have brought her all the way from the town.

Christian came to a quick decision. He turned to Manuel.

'We'll attack the camp from the front. You take the dynamite and place it in position behind the sheds.

'When will I start the fuses?' demanded Manuel.

'I'll give you the signal,' stated Christian. 'If you see that I've been injured or killed you must use your own initiative.'

'Can't we attack the camp in secret, just

taking out one of the enemy at a time?' asked one soldier.

'My sister has just been taken into Scarpia's tent by Jose,' snapped Christian. 'We haven't got time to make a secret attack. When I give the signal we all rush down the hill. Start firing as soon as you like. It will all help to create confusion.'

As he spoke he could see Alicia being led from Scarpia's tent. He hesitated before giving the signal in order to see where Jose was taking her. She was led to the end hut. That was where the Indian had said Rand was being held. At least he knew now exactly where he would be heading.

'All right,' he addressed the man again. 'I'll be heading for the end hut, the one where Lieutenant Rand is being held. The rest of you, kill every one of Scarpia's guards. Good luck.' He started to race down the hill.

In the end hut Jose pushed Alicia through the door. She expected to be met by her husband, but surely the person who was slumped in the chair wasn't Rand.

'What have you done to him?' she screamed.

The guard who was holding her was forced to tighten his grip on her arms.

'He's just happened to have a large dose of opium,' stated Jose.

'You swine.' She struggled with the guard, but he was too strong for her.

At that moment there was the sound of shooting from outside. Jose put his head out through the door.

'It seems that your friends are arriving, so we haven't much time.' He closed the door.

'What are you going to do?' demanded Alicia.

'I'm going to shoot him.' Jose nodded towards Rand. 'He's been a thorn in the flesh ever since he came into our camp. As to what's going to happen to you, that's your decision.'

'What do you mean?'

'Well, you can come back to the camp with

me. You're a very desirable woman.'

'I'll never come back with you. If Rand is going to die, then I'll die with him.'

'Very commendable, but a waste of womanhood. Still, it's your decision.'

At that moment Rand groaned.

'Ah, Sleeping Beauty is stirring,' observed Jose.

Rand not only opened his eyes, but he stood up.

'If I'm to die I want to be on my feet,' he said, slurring his words.

'If you insist,' said Jose. He turned his gun on Rand.

'Rand, I love you,' cried Alicia.

'I'm afraid we haven't got time for all that.' Jose prepared to shoot Rand. However he was having difficulty because Rand was swaying like a drunkard.

'For God's sake keep still,' shouted Jose.

But Rand was weaving from side to side and Jose couldn't get a clear shot at him. At one point Rand almost toppled over. He was forced to put his hand on the ground to steady himself. Jose waited impatiently for him to come upright. When Rand did it was with a swift movement that took Jose completely by surprise. Rand's next movement was even more surprising. He produced the knife which had been hidden in his boot. The knife found Jose's heart before Jose could take aim with his revolver.

As Jose slid to the floor the guard realized the precariousness of his position. He pushed Alicia away and went for his gun. Rand's reaction was quicker; he had picked up Jose's gun, and with it he shot the guard while he was still trying to draw his own.

At that moment Christian crashed through the door. He took in the situation.

'Thank God you're both safe. Scarpia has been killed and all his men have fled. They didn't have the stomach for a fight. Now we've got to get out of here. The huts will be blown up in a couple of minutes.'

They all dived out through the door. Alicia held Rand's hand as they ran.

'I thought you were drugged,' she gasped.

'That's what everybody thought. But I think the Indian girl watered down the drug. I drank the tequila, but there was hardly any opium in it.'

'Her name is Lily of the Valley,' supplied Christian.

They dived into a dry ditch. They were just in time because there was a series of huge bangs followed by the sight of the huts collapsing.

'Manuel did a good job,' Christian announced.

His observation went unnoticed by Rand and Alicia, who were locked in a passionate kiss.

When at last they broke free Rand asked her:

'How did you get here?'

'I had a premonition that you might be in danger. So I came.'

'She sometimes has premonitions,' Christian supplied.

Rand was about to kiss Alicia again when there was a sudden red glow on the horizon.

The three stood up and stared in wonder at the apparition.

'What on earth's that?' demanded Rand.

'It's the Apaches. They must be burning the poppy-fields. The women are working so hard in the poppy-fields that the men aren't getting their conjugal rights.'

Rand's reaction was to burst into laughter. Alicia glanced at him with surprise, then she too began to laugh. Soon Christian joined them. The three of them were laughing as though they'd never stop. The soldier who had come to announce that it was all over, shrugged when he saw them doubled up with laughter and walked away.

A couple of weeks later Rand was once again in Colonel Stanton's office.

'Sit down, Rand,' said the colonel. He was studying a report which he had picked up from his desk on Rand's entry.

Rand waited patiently. When the colonel finished the report he glanced up.

'This is very satisfactory. Very satisfactory.

You did an excellent job.'

'Thank you, sir.'

'You not only put the poppy-fields out of action for the foreseeable future but you also managed to kill the leader of the gang of outlaws. I have another report here from the acting mayor of Limos which says that the gang of outlaws won't cause any trouble in future.'

'I think Christian is quite right,' Rand supplied.

'There's one part I don't understand,' said the colonel, with a cough.

Rand waited for the inevitable question.

'It says here that you married this Christian Lorez's sister. Is that correct?'

'Yes, that's quite right, sir.'

The colonel subjected Rand to one of his stares.

'I suppose you'll be bringing her back here,' he said, eventually.

'No, sir. I've made up my mind to leave the army.'

Rand had expected a considerable reaction to the announcement. After all, in the colonel's eyes leaving the army voluntarily was almost akin to desertion. However, to his surprise, the colonel merely smiled.

'I assume you have other plans?'

'Yes, sir. The mayor of San Caldiz has asked me to draw maps of Mexico. It hasn't been done before. It's an exciting project.' For the first time there was a measure of excitement in Rand's voice.

The colonel tapped the report on his desk.

'I suppose this isn't the full story, is it?'

'No sir. There are some exciting details which I've missed out.'

The colonel went over to a drinks cabinet. 'Before you leave I want you to have a drink with me here. I'd be more than interested to hear about those exciting details. My daily routine is getting rather boring these days.'

'Well, there were one or two rather un-usual events...' Rand began.